'What is it with you?' Lawrence asked, each word a jagged chip of ice designed to pierce her defences. 'Why is it impossible for us to reach even the most basic of friendly relations?'

Kim smiled thinly. 'Could it be that I'm just not interested in you?'

'It could be,' Lawrence agreed silkily. 'But I have a feeling it goes deeper than that.'

'But then, of course, you would,' Kim jeered, hiding the sharp intake of her breath. 'Anything rather than accept there might be a woman in the world who doesn't think you're God's gift.'

Lawrence gave a short, humourless laugh. 'Oh, they exist. Fortunately, I just haven't met up with many of them.'

We hope you're enjoying our new addition to our Contemporary Romance series—stories which take a light-hearted look at the Zodiac and show that love can be written in the stars!

Every month you can get to know a different combination of star-crossed lovers, with one story that follows the fortunes of a hero or heroine when they embark on the romance of a lifetime with someone born under another sign of the Zodiac. This month features a sizzling love-affair between **Virgo** and **Gemini**.

To find out more fascinating facts about this month's featured star sign, turn to the back pages of this book. . .

ABOUT THIS MONTH'S AUTHOR

Shirley Kemp says: 'I'm a fairly typical Gemini, with a compulsive interest in life and an itch to travel. But what absorbs me most is people and what makes them tick. My main interests have been psychology, parapsychology, numerology, palmistry, tarot and—of course—astrology. From the study of all these things, I've come to believe that, while we shape our own destiny by the choices we make, there appears to be a set course; dictated by our own unique personality—a blend of many influences including the astrological—it makes some things almost inevitable.'

ON GOSSAMER WINGS

BY

SHIRLEY KEMP

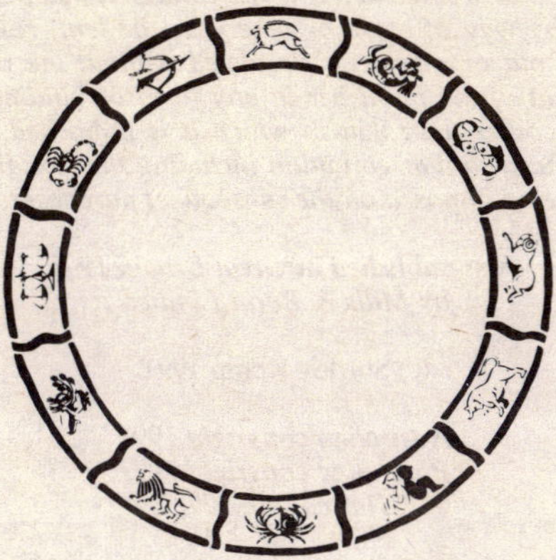

MILLS & BOON LIMITED
ETON HOUSE 18–24 PARADISE ROAD
RICHMOND SURREY TW9 1SR

First published in Great Britain 1991
by Mills & Boon Limited

This edition 1991

ISBN 0 263 77196 2

Set in 10 on 11½ pt Linotron Times
01-9108-52625 Z
Typeset in Great Britain by Centracet, Cambridge
Made and printed in Great Britain

CHAPTER ONE

DARK grey clouds scudded across the sky to gather ominously on the horizon. Large, round drops of moisture spattered suddenly against the windscreen of the car and Kimberley Harris groaned. Rain! The English summer weather had obviously followed her across the Channel into France.

Ten minutes later the rain had become torrential and when a sign for motorway services showed Kimberley turned off and drove into the car park. It was almost full and the parking space she eventually found was some distance from the long, low building.

The beautiful morning had lulled her into a sense of false optimism and her car, despite bulging at the seams with everything she'd deemed necessary for a two-week stay at the cottage, did not contain an umbrella.

There was nothing for it but to make a dash through the deluge.

'Ugh!' She groaned as the water seeped through her light jacket to run ticklishly against her skin. Thank goodness the weather was mild. The last thing she wanted now was to catch a heavy cold. Pam would never forgive her for turning up at her wedding to her 'gorgeous' Frenchman with a red nose.

She increased her speed and had just reached the entrance when she collided with someone running in from another direction. The impact knocked the breath from her body. As she tottered backwards, strong arms were flung about her, holding her steady against a hard, muscular chest.

'Oh, lord! I'm sorry,' a deep male voice apologised. 'I had my head down and didn't see you.'

The arms remained around her, and Kim moved irritably to disentangle herself.

'You can let me go now.'

'Sorry,' he apologised again, carefully releasing his hold on her. 'Are you hurt?'

With water running from her hair into her eyes, it was difficult for Kim to see the owner of the voice. Peering up, she got the impression of a tall man, but his features were blurred by her attempts to blink away the water. A mop of dark curls glistened above a broad forehead and Kim thought fleetingly that his hair was too long.

And then, as she continued to look, she got a jolt which affected her balance far more than the collision.

Perhaps it was the blurred vision, but, for a moment, she was looking again at Philip Crossley. Her heart turned a somersault, and she felt the blood drain away from her face.

She shook her head to clear it, and slowly his face came into focus. He had the height, the same dark hair as Philip, but his face, with its strong lean lines, bore no resemblance to that of the man who had broken her heart. Gradually her pulse came back to normal.

The stranger's face was full of concern as she continued to stare at him.

'Are you OK?' he asked worriedly. 'You look as though you've seen a ghost.'

Which wasn't far from the truth, she thought a little wildly. Philip Crossley was a phantom she'd thought successfully buried in the past.

From somewhere, she dredged up some self-control

and gave him a perfunctory smile. 'Once I get my breath back, I'll be fine.'

'Are you sure?'

'I wouldn't have said so if I wasn't.'

She shot him a critical look. He was handsome, despite the length of his hair, and the amber colour of his eyes was quite distinctive. They smiled engagingly into hers.

'You're drenched,' he said sympathetically. 'Let me get you something warm. . .a cup of tea or coffee, perhaps?'

Kim felt the prickle of tension along her spine which always warned her when a man was more than casually interested.

'That won't be necessary,' she said stiffly, knowing her face flamed. 'If you'll just let me pass. . . I'd like to get to the cloakroom.'

She pushed past him hastily, surprised to find she was shaking—probably the effects of the shock. . .and her temporary hallucination. Damn the man for reminding her! She swore silently.

The cloakroom was crammed with women and Kim had difficulty finding a corner of a mirror for her to survey the damage to her appearance.

How many of her employees would recognise their usually pin-neat managing director now? she wondered, peering at her dripping hair, pale face and smudged mascara. She looked like the proverbial drowned rat and felt even worse.

Determinedly, she dried her thick brown hair as best she could with paper towels, and brushed it into some semblance of order. Then, with a hand that still trembled slightly, she reapplied her light make-up.

A hot cup of tea seemed suddenly a matter of life or death.

The motorway-services restaurant was heaving with damp travellers taking refuge from the downpour.

With sandwiches in one hand and a large cup of tea in the other, Kim stood uncertainly, scanning the room for a seat. She felt uncharacteristically self-conscious standing alone among all these strangers, and the sight of a familiar figure came almost as a relief.

He was standing with his back to her, talking to a man and a woman, and she was able to appraise him coolly. He'd taken off his wet jacket and she could see that his shoulders were broad, his figure taut and powerful in close-fitting jeans and sweatshirt. His dark hair still glistened with raindrops trapped in the springy curls.

A table beside him became suddenly vacant, and he moved into it with his friends.

He was facing her now, engrossed in conversation, and she was able to study him surreptitiously. Apart from his height and colouring, she realised, he wasn't at all like Philip Crossley.

He looked up suddenly and caught her staring at him.

Too late for her to avert her gaze now, she decided, holding what her friend Pam called her 'aloof Virgo stare' on his smiling face.

He waved a friendly hand to her, indicating the vacant seat beside him, but she turned pointedly away.

He was probably hoping their little collision might lead to other things, and she wasn't about to encourage him in that.

A small table for two was vacant in the far corner and she moved towards it thankfully, sitting so that her back was to the body of the room. She would offer herself no temptation to repeat her mistake, she vowed grimly.

She'd eaten one of her sandwiches and was just beginning on the other when she felt a light touch on her shoulder and looked up into his bright amber gaze.

'Are you feeling all right?'

Without invitation, he lowered his tall frame into the seat opposite her. Kim felt her hackles rise and was tempted to be sarcastic and invite him to sit, but decided it would be water off a duck's back.

'No broken bones or anything?' he went on enquiringly, seemingly unaware of her antagonism.

'Obviously not,' she replied with asperity. 'Otherwise I'd hardly be sitting here drinking tea and eating my sandwiches.'

He raised dark brows at her, a spark of amusement glinting in his gold-flecked eyes.

'You still haven't forgiven me, I see.' He touched her fingers, which had been drumming unconsciously on the table. 'Is there some way I could make amends?'

Kim pulled her hand away as the unexpectedly electric current of his personality set up strange tingling sensations through her body.

'If you want me to say I forgive you. . .then I do,' she said evenly, trying to keep some perspective on her feelings of hostility. It wasn't his fault she'd mistaken him for someone else. She went on a little less sharply, 'And there's no need for amends. It was an accident. No harm done. Nothing more to say.'

'Ah!' That maddening lift of his brows had Kim almost grinding her teeth.

'OK. Well, in that case, I won't mention it again.'

'Good!' Kim lowered her eyes from his and drank from her cup. It was a gesture of dismissal, but he seemed impervious. Kim thought grimly that he must have a hide like a rhinoceros's.

'But there's no reason why we can't talk about something else, is there?'

Kimberley tossed her hair back in an unconsciously nervous gesture. She'd met a number of handsome men since Philip and none had made even the smallest dent in her carefully constructed armour. It was disturbing to find this stranger had the ability to get under her skin. . .even if it was only to irritate rather than fascinate.

'I can't see what else we have to talk about.'

'We could talk about you,' he said. 'For instance, are you in France on business or for a holiday?'

His eyes were a peculiar shade of hazel, almost amber, and Kim felt his scrutiny with a sense of unease. Despite his easygoing approach, she had a feeling he was a man to be reckoned with.

'We could. Only I don't propose to discuss my private affairs with you.'

'You're in France to have an affair?'

The amused gleam in his eyes invited her to share his teasing joke.

Kim deliberately pulled down the corners of her full mouth.

'If I am, it's my business,' she told him coldly.

He frowned, watching her through narrowed lids, the dark fringe of his lashes giving him a mysterious air.

'I don't think you're having an affair,' he said consideringly. 'I was watching you on the ferry. And, if I may say so, you have the look of a woman who has yet to be awakened.'

Kim gasped. His familiarity was almost insulting.

The infernal cheek of the man. To think he'd been staring at her on the ferry and she hadn't known. He'd been aware of her even before she'd known he existed. A shiver ran through her.

'What are you, then?' she demanded tightly. 'A professional psychiatrist? Or perhaps a *talented* amateur?'

To her fury, he laughed aloud at her outburst.

'That's better,' he said. 'Now *you're* showing an interest in *me*.'

She gritted her teeth. 'I assure you I'm not the smallest bit interested in you. And I'd be glad if you'd go away at once and leave me in peace to finish my food.'

He sighed. 'Why are you so defensive? Don't you like to be friendly?'

'Only with my friends.'

He eyed her critically, and Kim had the feeling he was beginning to dislike what he saw.

Good, she thought irritably. If he disliked her enough, maybe he'd go away.

'If everybody has to work this hard to get to know you. . .' his deep voice had a hard edge '. . .I'm surprised you *have* any friends.'

Kim laughed shortly. 'It may come as a shock to you to find I don't care a damn what surprises you.'

'That's your prerogative.'

He shrugged, quite unperturbed, and then went on, as though they were having a pleasant discussion, 'What part of France are you headed for?'

'That's my business.'

He made a brief impatient sound. 'It could be mine also, if you were travelling my way.'

Kim stared at him in astonishment. 'You're not going to suggest we travel together, are you?'

He shrugged. 'It's an idea, if we're both going in the same direction.'

Her cup came down into her saucer with a crash. 'Even if your journey matched mine inch for inch,' she gritted, her breath shortened by indignation, 'there's no way I would ever dream of giving you a lift.'

He fixed her with an unsettling stare.

She stared back, surprised to find that her heart was pounding uncomfortably.

'Pity,' he said. 'Because dreams can sometimes be a foretaste of reality.'

He smiled suddenly, an indentation appearing in his cheek. It gave him an unexpectedly disarming look, which only made her dislike him more. He was obviously well aware of the strength of his charm.

'And some dreams turn into nightmares,' she said icily.

'True,' he agreed, eyeing her narrowly. 'And, for a woman alone, travelling can sometimes be hazardous. It could be a definite advantage to have me as a passenger.'

Kim snorted derisively. 'You mean, to act as a deterrent against intrusive strangers, no doubt.'

The snub couldn't have been more obvious, but he seemed impervious.

'Could be.' His amber eyes gave nothing away. 'A beautiful woman, in any situation, is bound to attract attention.'

'And sometimes it's the wrong sort,' Kim said testily, ignoring the implied compliment. If one tactic didn't work, he was obviously prepared to try another. 'Nice try,' she jeered, 'but it didn't work.'

He shrugged. 'Can't win them all.'

Kim ground her teeth. He had a snappy answer for everything and she was tired of the effort to come out on top.

She stood up. 'Since you obviously don't intend to go, I will.'

'Ah! Shame!' He shrugged, maddeningly cool. 'Are you sure you don't want a little company on your journey?'

She glared at him. 'You really don't give up, do you?'

He said calmly, 'Not easily. No.'

'Neither do I.' Kim picked up her jacket and bag. 'Goodbye. I hope you have better luck elsewhere.' She smiled, deliberately condescending. 'I'm sure you will eventually.'

He looked up at her coolly. 'I never trust to luck. I believe in making my own.'

His expression was unnerving, as though he had just made a vow.

She left without looking back, but felt his gaze on her the whole way to the exit.

The rain had eased to a thin drizzle and, putting her jacket over her head and shoulders, Kim ran for her car, sighing with relief as she opened the door and got in behind the wheel. The sprint had seemed like a dash for freedom, but from what was she running? Whatever it was, she'd made her escape, she thought with a sense of relief.

But her relief was short-lived. Her getaway wasn't as speedy as she'd hoped.

Everybody seemed to be leaving at the same time and she groaned as the long queue in front of her ground to a halt on the slip-road.

She felt suddenly impatient to arrive at the hotel she had booked to stay in overnight, and longed for the luxury of a deep, hot bath.

With a bit of luck, she would be at the cottage by

tomorrow afternoon, and would have a day or two to settle in before the wedding.

The traffic had begun to move slowly and she pushed the gear-stick into first with a sigh of relief.

The sigh became a groan as a familiar figure passed by her window, broad shoulders hunched against the rain.

She found herself crouching down in her seat, as though that would prevent him from seeing her, and she straightened with a small sound of annoyance. Why did she have such a feeling of inevitability about this pushy stranger? Nothing was inevitable. All she had to do was ignore him.

He was there, a little further on, standing on the verge, a rain-soaked bag beside him and his thumb raised.

From the corner of her eye, she saw that he was looking in her direction.

Did he actually think she would give him a lift? In this day and age, when the papers were full of. . .?

She picked up the newspaper on the passenger-seat and opened it at random, lifting the pages so that they hid her face.

She found herself staring at the astrology section and, almost automatically, her eyes sought her birth sign. Under Virgo, the astrologer had predicted that 'a stranger's act of kindness could be the beginning of a beautiful friendship.'

She laughed aloud, and then stifled the sound with her hand.

Had he heard? she wondered worriedly.

Cautiously, she peered around the edges of the paper. He was still there, thumb raised, hoping for an 'act of kindness'.

Perhaps he was a Virgo too, she thought with a strange little giggle, and ducked back behind her paper.

Giving this stranger a lift would be more an act of madness than of kindness, she thought ironically.

The traffic was moving again.

Kim discarded the paper and, looking resolutely ahead, she drove past the hitch-hiker, filtering out on to the motorway with an inexplicable feeling of relief.

Why, she asked herself, did she have this feeling of having avoided, by the skin of her teeth, something which had seemed inevitable?

Kimberley settled into the flow of the traffic. She was tired now and the steady pace of the slow lane was more appealing even than saving an hour or so of daylight.

She was looking forward to seeing Pam, but not particularly to all the preamble to the wedding.

It was still difficult to realise that her friend was going to be married. It was only a few months ago that she had been nagging Kim to share the French cottage she'd booked for six months' holiday.

'Six months!' Kim had exclaimed in disbelief. 'I doubt if I could manage six *days* at the moment. When you're running a business, you can't just get up and go at the drop of a hat.'

'Rubbish!' Pam had said firmly. 'Gordon Brown could run the place for you with one hand tied behind his back.'

Not entirely true, Kim thought wryly, but near enough.

A loud bang jolted Kim's nervous system, bringing her sharply back to the present. The sudden wrenching movement of the steering-wheel had her heart beating with terror. She hung on grimly, but the car seemed uncannily to take control of itself, swerving dizzily, mounting the grass verge and then, as Kim jerked on the wheel, dropping back down on to the hard shoulder. More as an automatic reflex than sensible action, she slammed her foot hard on the brake and the vehicle shuddered violently to a stop.

It was long moments before her heart slowed its painful hammering against her ribs and she was able to breathe again and collect her wits enough to realise that she'd burst a tyre.

She slumped back in her seat and took a long slow breath to calm her nerves.

She had a spare wheel, of course, and the necessary tools and jack somewhere in the boot. All she had to do was put into practice the lesson her father had given her on the intricacies of changing a wheel.

Easier said than done. She groaned as she remembered that, even under her father's close supervision, she hadn't managed to make much of a job of it. As boss of her own engineering company, she ought to be ashamed to admit it, but she was hopeless with machinery. Still, all she could do was try.

Reluctantly, she opened the car door and got out. She opened up the boot and groaned. Two cases and a number of small bags filled the space and would have to be removed before she could find what she needed.

Her heart sank.

If she were the stereotypical female, she might be tempted to stand helplessly by and appeal to the chivalry of passing motorists, but it went against the grain to conform to the expected, and grimly she began lifting the luggage out.

It was raining heavily again now and as she bent over the boot her jacket took another drenching. She had a moment of panic as she wondered if the spare tyre was serviceable enough, but it looked all right as she hauled it out on to the ground.

The nuts on the wheel, however, defied all her efforts to unlock them, and at last she was forced to admit defeat. Dirt-streaked and near to uncharacteristic tears, she threw the tool down and stood up to stretch her aching back.

'Here! Come out of the way and let me.'

Strong hands moved her aside and she felt the flooding of relief.

She turned with a smile on her face, but he was already stooping. Kim stared at the dark curling hair as he bent in concentration, torn between relief and aggravation. Why did it have to be him?

Chagrined, she noted how easily the nuts moved beneath the pressure of his lean hands. It took only minutes for him to complete the job and release the jack.

'There's a knack to it.' He grinned briefly as he straightened and caught sight of her expression. 'That, and the application of a little elbow-grease.'

Kim frowned. Why was it that even when he was being helpful he managed somehow to annoy her?

'I'm afraid I don't happen to carry much elbow-grease around with me,' she said icily.

He looked irritated. 'In that case, it's just as well that I do.' He was wiping his hands on a cloth. His easy grin had vanished. 'And you might try showing a little gratitude.'

Kim bit her lip, wondering why she felt his help to be more of an affront than a favour.

'I didn't ask. You offered,' she said tightly, smothering a small inner sense of shame. If he'd been any other man, she would have called him a Good Samaritan.

Her 'Good Samaritan' fixed her with a steely stare.

'And already I'm regretting it. I should have left you to stew.'

'Perhaps you should,' Kim shot back, meeting his grim look with a defiant toss of her head. 'I'd have managed myself eventually.'

His laugh was mirthless and derisive. 'I wouldn't take any bets on that, Miss Independent What's-your-name.'

'Miss Harris,' Kim said quellingly. 'If you're going to use my name—get it right. It's Kimberley Harris.'

He didn't even acknowledge the put-down, his whole attention seemingly on the task of wiping his hands free of grease. Deep lines were stubbornly etched each side of his mouth, thinning the sensual contours.

Kim's scalp prickled. Despite the apparently easy-going manner he'd displayed initially, she sensed that here was a man who would be hard to overcome.

She seethed with indignation as he continued to ignore her. 'You might at least make a pretence of manners by introducing yourself.'

He looked up at last, his eyes fixed narrowly on her flushed and angry face. 'I didn't think you'd be interested,' he said coolly. 'My name's Lawrence Cory. Does that mean anything to you?'

She frowned. 'No. Should it?'

'Not necessarily,' he said enigmatically, and she could have hit him.

She would have liked to challenge him on the meaning of that cryptic remark, but knew it would only encourage him. 'You seem to enjoy playing games,' she said icily. 'Unfortunately I don't, so, if you've finished doing the job, I'll say thank you and goodbye.'

'I haven't quite.' He bent to retrieve the damaged

wheel. 'Despite your churlishness, I'll carry on. I'm a man who always likes to finish what I've started.'

'My churlishness. . .' she began, then stopped. This was just the kind of childish interchange he was hoping for. She closed her lips firmly and saw his thin smile of cynical amusement.

Silently, she watched him stow the wheel away in the boot.

'Get a new tyre on that as soon as you can,' he ordered as he covered the wheel and began putting the luggage back into the boot. 'You never know when you might need it.'

'Something I've just learned to my cost,' she said grimly.

'Precisely. And I might not be around next time to rescue you.'

'Mercifully true,' Kim murmured *sotto voce* and then crossed her fingers in superstitious hope that there would never be a next time. One experience of a burst tyre was enough for one lifetime. And being rescued by Lawrence Cory was more than enough.

The last piece of luggage was stowed and he slammed the boot shut.

Kim's spirits rose. Any minute now she would be waving him goodbye, so she could afford to be happy.

'I really am grateful you came along when you did, but I won't keep you any longer.'

She looked around. There wasn't a parked car anywhere in sight.

'But how on earth did you get here?' she demanded. 'You're hitch-hiking, aren't you?'

'So you did notice me thumbing earlier on,' he said. 'Why didn't you stop?'

'You must be joking,' she asserted derisively. 'I make it a firm rule never to pick up hitch-hikers.'

He laughed unpleasantly. 'Well, you're going to have to pick one up now, I'm afraid. I had a lift this far, but my benefactors couldn't wait. They've gone on.'

Kim stared at him in consternation. 'Why couldn't they wait? It only took a moment.'

'They were in a hurry.' He shrugged dismissively. 'Besides, they weren't really going my way.'

'Well, maybe I'm not either,' she argued, beginning to feel apprehensive.

If it hadn't been for the fact that it was *her* tyre which had burst so inopportunely, she would have sworn that somehow he had stage-managed this whole situation.

'Where *are* you going?' he asked.

Kim named her destination and the village where she intended to stop overnight.

'Fine!' He nodded calmly. 'That's right on my way.'

Kim bit her lip, vexed at her own stupidity. She should have asked him first where he was going—and she had a strong suspicion that the answer might have been very different.

'It looks as though you're stuck with me,' he said ironically.

She looked helplessly at the passing traffic. 'Perhaps someone else might pick you up,' she suggested a little desperately. 'If you put up your thumb.'

'And perhaps not,' he said grimly. 'Meanwhile, I don't intend to get any wetter.'

He put his hand determinedly on the handle of the passenger door. 'I've helped you out of a spot. Now it's your turn.'

The rain had eased again, but they were both soaked through.

Kim bit her lip uncertainly.

'Oh, get in, woman!' he said irritably, taking her by

the elbow and steering her around to the driver's door. 'And stop worrying. I'm perfectly harmless.'

'Forgive me if I don't take *your* word for that,' Kim growled in temper as she shook herself free of his hold.

But there seemed nothing else to do.

Damn the rain. Damn her burst tyre. And damn him, she muttered resentfully beneath her breath. But cursing him wouldn't make him disappear.

Dangerous as it obviously was, she would have to give him the lift he requested, she accepted with resignation. Fortunately, the hotel she was heading for wasn't that much further away.

'OK,' she said grudgingly. 'Let's get into the car before we drown.'

'Most kind of you to worry about me,' he mocked, an ironic gleam in his amber eyes.

'I'm not worried,' she responded sourly. 'I'm sure you can take care of yourself.'

He nodded, but said nothing, simply indicating his bag with a questioning lift of his dark brows.

'Squeeze it in there if you can.' Kim pointed to the boot. 'It's too wet to go inside.'

She got into the car and opened the passenger door for him.

Her own jacket was soaked and she took it off and threw it on the floor in the back. It was probably ruined, she thought ruefully. But that was the least of her worries at the moment.

She heard the thump of the boot's lid being lowered and then Lawrence Cory was getting in beside her, his long legs taking up all the available space beneath the dashboard.

His thigh brushed hers and she moved pointedly away.

With a sigh, he settled deeper into his seat, taking care to make no further contact with her.

They were back out on to the motorway and had travelled some distance before either of them spoke again.

He broke the silence. 'Why do I get the impression you don't like me?'

She shot him a guarded look.

'I don't *dislike* you,' she said, after a brief pause. 'I don't know you.'

'And don't want to know me either, if your attitude is anything to go by.'

She laughed shortly. 'Does it surprise you that not every woman is willing to be chatted up by any man on the slightest pretext?'

He grimaced. 'I wasn't trying to chat you up. Are you always so suspicious?'

'Always,' Kim affirmed with a nod. 'If you weren't trying to chat me up at the motorway services, what *were* you doing?'

'I was showing natural concern for having bumped into you,' he said exasperatedly. 'Strange though it may seem, I was worried that I might have hurt you. I'm a pretty hefty guy to bump into.'

Kim laughed shortly. 'Then I must be tougher than I look, because it didn't hurt a bit.'

He nodded. 'But nothing like as tough as you'd like to be.'

She felt his eyes on her and was tempted to meet his gaze, but went on looking straight ahead.

'It would be intriguing to know why that is.'

'Am I getting the amateur psychiatrist bit again?' she asked bitterly. 'Don't you know it's offensive?'

'It isn't meant to be,' he replied calmly. 'Most people

like to feel they're interesting. What makes you so different?'

'I don't know,' she said, shooting him a hostile glance. 'But I'd be glad if you'd kindly accept that I am and keep your analyses to yourself.'

'I think I'll agree on that,' he said coolly. 'The effort is only worth the results and, with you, I don't seem to be getting any.'

He sighed again and settled himself more comfortably, his broad frame seeming to take up all the available space. His shoulder brushed hers and, this time, it was he who moved away.

His gesture irritated her already sensitised nerves.

She felt his gaze on her and turned to find that he was appraising her openly. Unembarrassed, he held her gaze, and it was she who looked away, flustered, and with a tinge of warm colour in her cheeks.

She felt the heat of his thigh only inches from her own. The male vitality of him seemed suddenly to fill the enclosed atmosphere of the car. Her body responded alarmingly with a tremor and, for some reason, she found it difficult to breathe. . .sensations so new to her that they threw her into confusion.

Here she was, with a complete stranger she'd been practically forced to accept as a passenger, and she was allowing him to affect her as if she were an impressionable schoolgirl. In fact a schoolgirl would have had more sense than to put herself into this stupid and potentially dangerous situation.

Not that she seemed to be in any danger at the moment. His withdrawal was almost tangible and, strangely, she found this almost as annoying as his verbal intrusion.

Unable to resist the urge, she shot him a quick glance and was relieved to see that his eyes were closed.

She prayed they would stay that way, at least until she had her strangely volatile feelings under control.

Shock was a peculiar thing, she reasoned as she deepened her breathing and tried consciously to relax, and within the space of an hour or so she'd had a double helping. It was hardly surprising, therefore, that she should be showing the effects.

She consoled herself with the thought that her stop-over hotel wasn't much further on. When she arrived, she would be able to get rid of her unwanted passenger for good.

CHAPTER TWO

THE hotel was set back off the road and, heavy-eyed with fatigue, Kim almost missed the turning off.

She had never been so relieved to arrive at her destination in her life.

'Oh, good! We've arrived.' Lawrence Cory stirred beside her.

'Yes.' Kim eyed him irritably. 'You can get out now.'

He'd been sleeping for most of the journey and looked annoyingly rested and alert, which was more than she could say for herself.

She got out stiffly and went around to open the boot.

'Leave the baggage to me.' Lawrence Cory was standing beside her.

'Thanks! But don't bother. I'll manage,' she said edgily.

'It's no bother,' he said stubbornly, elbowing her aside. 'After your kindness in giving me a lift, it's the least I can do.'

Kim thought dully that she could do without this. Why couldn't the man just go? she asked herself vexedly. His presence now was an embarrassment. He'd helped her and she'd helped him in return. She had no further responsibility towards him and she didn't want him to feel any towards her.

'Just leave it,' she insisted, but she might have saved her breath.

He walked away from her, carrying her cases, and she had no option but to follow him up the steps and into Reception.

The lobby was small, but gleamed with polished wood and clean marbled floors.

Ignoring Lawrence Cory, who had dropped the cases and was standing alongside her, she introduced herself to the dapper little man behind the reception desk.

'I'm Kimberley Harris. I've booked a room for the night.'

'Ah! Mademoiselle Harris. I am Monsieur Dubois. Welcome,' he said expansively. 'We have your room ready for you. I hope you will like it.'

'Thank you, *monsieur*. I'm sure I will.'

Kim answered him in French which had become a little rusty with disuse, but he beamed with pleasure.

A brass bell stood in pride of place on his desk and he hit it with a flourish. 'Henri will come to take up your baggage.'

'That won't be necessary. I'll carry the cases up.'

In contrast to her own, Lawrence Cory's French was perfect, and somehow that only increased her annoyance at his unwarranted interruption.

Monsieur Dubois was looking in a startled way from one to the other.

'Ah! Am I to take it you will require a. . .double room. . .*mademoiselle*?'

Kim flushed scarlet. 'No! I won't,' she said grimly. 'Mr. . .Cory. . .is a. . .friend. . .' It would be too complicated to explain the true situation, she decided irritably, and settled for this little deviation from the truth. 'He won't be staying. He's travelling on.'

Kim's glare defied Lawrence Cory to make any comment.

'You can leave my luggage to Henri,' she said. 'I'd much prefer to say goodbye to you here.'

She held out her hand to him and, after a pause, he took it.

There was no mistaking the mockery in his eyes as he bent to kiss her hand. 'I hate goodbyes,' he said. 'I'd rather say *au revoir*.'

Henri was waiting at the tiny gilded cage of a lift.

'*Au revoir*, then,' she said, trying to keep the waspishness out of her voice, adding, as a gesture of goodwill, 'and *bon voyage*.'

He acknowledged this sally with a wry nod of his head, but made no further comment.

She walked to the lift without even a backward glance. There was no need for thanks. . .they had each discharged their debt.

He still stood there, a cold kind of humour gleaming in his strange amber eyes, watching as the little open cage ascended.

Lawrence Cory was gone, but, strangely, so had her fatigue.

She'd planned to relax, but instead she found herself pacing the room, her nerves wound up tighter than a drum.

Even in the bath, she couldn't lie still. The peculiar tension was there to spoil her enjoyment. But it was impossible to say what the tension was, unless it was the result of a tiring and unconventional day.

She gave herself a mental shake. Why was she even bothering to conjecture about him? He was gone. . .ships that pass, and all that. . .so what did it matter?

Her stomach rumbled inelegantly.

Heavens! She was suddenly ravenous.

She didn't linger in the bath as she'd planned. Her odd impatience made the hot water uncomfortable. Better to get out and dry and cure her hunger with food. Perhaps then she would be able to relax.

She brushed her hair to gleaming obedience and applied a little light make-up to her inexplicably glowing face.

She rummaged in a case and brought out her favourite short cocktail dress of midnight-blue, which accentuated the brilliant blue of her eyes. It had thin shoulder straps and was wonderfully cut to accommodate her curves. She had always looked good in it and wore it whenever she needed to boost her confidence.

Though why it should need a boost now was a mystery. She was only going down to dinner in an unpretentious little hotel. . .something she'd done so many times before without even thinking about it.

As she put the finishing touches to her appearance with a pair of blue pendant earrings, a light knock sounded on the door.

Puzzled, Kim opened it, and was instantly tempted to shut it again. . .into Lawrence Cory's handsome face. She resisted the impulse and instead she stared at him, her mouth open in unguarded astonishment. He looked fantastic. Somewhere from his rain-soaked bag he'd extracted a creaseless lightweight grey suit and immaculate pale blue shirt, which seemed incredible in the circumstances. A darker tie exactly matched the charcoal-grey of his gleaming shoes.

'What on earth are you doing here?' she demanded a little breathlessly. 'I thought you'd be well on your way by now.'

He gave a short laugh. 'You mean you *hoped* I would be.'

She shrugged. 'It makes no difference to me.'

'Good,' he said. 'In that case you'll be pleased to hear that I've got a room on the floor above.'

He was attractive, she had to admit; incredibly so, and it made her angry. Men like him always thought they were irresistible. Fortunately, all he aroused in her was a strong feeling of irritation.

But she felt threatened by his persistence. 'Is this some kind of a game?' she demanded frostily.

'A game.' His eyes narrowed on her face. 'Why should I be playing a game?'

'I don't know,' Kim answered him with mounting anger. 'But if it has anything to do with me then you're wasting your time.'

He frowned. 'I hope not. I came to ask you to have dinner with me.'

She shook her head. 'I don't think so. I was just about to ring room-service and have them bring up some sandwiches.'

'Dressed like that?' His amber eyes swept over her with undisguised approval, taking in the firm high bosom, the trim waist and slim gentle curve of her hips. 'What a waste that would be.'

Kim returned his ironically admiring glance with a look of cold fury. Why had he remained here to disturb and unsettle her feelings? Until now, she hadn't acknowledged how much of a relief his departure had been.

'I can do without the sexist remarks,' she said bitterly.

She saw his back stiffen.

'If it's sexist to let you know you're a beautiful and desirable woman, then I suppose I was being sexist. I apologise. I won't make that mistake again.'

'I'm glad to hear it,' Kim said evenly, but with a feeling that she had somehow lost rather than won a point in the battle.

He returned her glare for a long moment before his expression changed to one of exasperation. 'Look, why don't we bury the hatchet?' He gave her a tentative smile. 'Today's my birthday. My invitation to dinner was by way of a celebration.'

'Your birthday!' Kim frowned suspiciously. 'Is this another of your games?'

'Here we go again.' His smile vanished, a cold glittering look taking its place. 'Can't you ever take anything at face value? I'm getting a little tired of my role as a seduction artist.'

'And I'm tired of your annoying persistence. So, why don't you just go away?' Kim spat back, fired by his anger. 'And as for dinner. . . I'd prefer to eat alone.'

The hardness of his expression might have daunted her had she not been so angry.

'What is it with you?' he asked, each word a jagged chip of ice designed to pierce her defences. 'Why is it impossible for us to reach even the most basic of friendly relations?'

Kim smiled thinly. 'Could it be that I'm just not interested in you?'

'It could be,' he agreed, silkily offensive. 'But I have a feeling it goes deeper than that.'

'But then, of course, you would,' Kim jeered, hiding the sharp intake of her breath. 'Anything, rather than accept there might be a woman in the world who doesn't think you're God's gift.'

He gave a short humourless laugh. 'Oh, they exist. Fortunately, I just haven't met up with many of them.'

'Well, you've met one now,' Kim said through clenched teeth, at a loss to understand the strength of her own hostility. 'Now perhaps you'll go and allow me to shut my door.'

She made to close the door against him. His tight, furious face stopped her halfway.

His eyes glittered coldly. 'My pleasure,' he said grimly. 'If that's the way you want it, that's the way you'll damned well get it. I've never had to force my company on a woman before and I don't intend to begin with you.'

The granite expression and white lines of fury about his mouth told her that, at last, she'd managed to penetrate his thick skin, but somehow she felt little satisfaction.

'Thank you,' she replied a little faintly.

He acknowledged her thanks with a cold mocking salute. 'I wish you joy of your solitary meal.'

His hard expression told her that joy was the last thing he wished her, but she consoled herself with the knowledge that he'd at last got the message.

He turned and walked away, denying her the chance to slam the door in his face.

She slammed it anyway, with all the force of her frustration. He'd had the last word and that fact added gall to the already bitter taste of their encounter.

Her breathing was harsh with the remnants of her anger, and she felt sorely tempted to fling herself on the bed and weep her temper away. Instead, she sat on the side of the bed trying to rationalise her feelings.

He was impossible. Arrogant, self-satisfied, overbearing. . .

But, at some level, she had to acknowledge her own uncompromising part in the battle that had been waged almost unavoidably between them.

Where did all this anger come from?

Some of it from the past, she admitted painfully, and she'd tried to make allowances for that. For a brief moment, Lawrence Cory had reminded her of Philip, and the ghosts had risen, along with the bitterness which she'd thought had burned itself out. But, as he had seen intuitively, it was more than that. Somehow,

Lawrence Cory represented a threat that was very much of the present.

Fate was unfair, she thought disconsolately, to link her with the only man who had been able to penetrate the comfortable wall she'd painstakingly constructed around her heart, albeit with only negative emotions. She despised his good looks, saw cynically through his charm, was angered by his attempts to coerce her into liking him. But even that was more emotion than any man had been capable of arousing in her during the past four years.

Uncharacteristic tears pricked at the back of her eyes, but she brushed them determinedly away. There was no way she was going to allow her brush with a stranger to upset her well-earned holiday.

She took up the newspaper she'd brought with her and sat in the deep armchair. But somehow the news seemed stale and uninteresting.

Before she knew it, her mind was back to Lawrence Cory. Was it really his birthday?

She looked at the date at the top of the paper. The third of June. What star sign did that make him?

She laughed shortly in self-derision. Pamela's obsession with astrology was beginning to get to her.

Nevertheless, she turned again to the horoscope section and looked up the date. A birthday today would make him a Gemini. The prediction was more detailed than the rest, since his sign was the topical one. She read with unwilling interest.

> For talented, multi-faceted Gemini, the year ahead is destined to be one of your most memorable. More than one major decision will have to be made shortly and in more than one area. Dominant career issues could conflict with a new and engrossing love-affair. Sparks may fly, but keep a cool head.

Kim snorted cynically. Talented Lawrence Cory might be; multi-faceted he certainly was, since she'd already seen more than one side to his seemingly versatile nature.

And romance, so it would appear, was on the cards for him as well as herself.

She read the prediction for her own sign of Virgo again, with its promise of a love-affair arising from a good turn performed by a stranger.

Odd, she mused, how the horoscopes, concocted no doubt in some newspaper office, probably by some junior reporter, seemed sometimes to verge on the truth.

Almost, but not quite, she thought cynically. Her *kind* stranger had departed with a flea in his ear, no doubt to lick his wounded pride and begin his search for a new and engrossing love-affair.

She wished him joy of it, though it seemed as though he might be in for a rough ride.

She put the paper from her irritably and stood up, brushing the creases from her dress.

Hunger pangs were gnawing persistently at her insides, so it was decision time. Was she going to skulk in her room eating a plate of uninteresting sandwiches, or was she going to exert her right to a decent meal in the dining-room?

Stubborn pride dictated her choice.

Kim stood in the doorway of the dining-room, her eyes scanning apprehensively. If he was there, she would leave immediately and have sandwiches brought up to her room. But he was nowhere to be seen. With a bit of luck, he might have decided to cut his losses and move on.

She smiled as a waiter came to direct her to a discreet

corner table, and sat back in her seat to survey the other guests, who appeared to be mainly middle-aged couples, retired people with time to spare for a slow holiday. In addition, there was one family with three small children, and two women in their fifties, presumably travelling alone.

As Kim idly watched, the larger of the two women looked up towards the doorway, with an expression of intense interest. An excited smile lit her face and she nudged her friend, who looked up with a little gasp of astonishment.

Kim followed the direction of their gaze and groaned.

Lawrence Cory had just entered and was crossing the dining-room, apparently coming straight towards her. Her heart leapt into nervous activity as she steeled herself for another inevitable confrontation. There was no way she was going to share a dinner table with him.

But, to her surprise, he walked past her table to another, in a secluded alcove, without even the acknowledgement of a glance.

He sat profile-on to her, but she glared at him none the less.

She had told him, in no uncertain terms, that she wished to be alone, but was peeved by the fact that he was so ostentatiously giving her her wish. Was this his unsubtle way of teaching her a lesson? she wondered indignantly. The conceit of the man! Did he really believe he had it in his power to punish her?

It was surely *she* who should be ignoring *him*. If she hadn't already ordered, she would have left and gone to her room, but it would be too embarrassing to do so now. And, in a way, it would be a defeat for her. . .another victory for him.

She set her chin firmly. She would stay and eat her dinner even if it choked her.

Determinedly, she looked across the room at him, ready to glare her defiance, but he was absorbed in studying the menu. She looked resentfully away. He wasn't even going to afford her the satisfaction of a challenge.

She allowed herself a cynical laugh. Why couldn't she simply accept the truth? Now he knew there was no chance of seduction, he'd completely lost interest. Wasn't that how it always went with men like him? If the conquest didn't come easily, the quest was soon abandoned. Having learned that painful lesson once, she was damned if she'd learn it all over again.

The food was delicious, but she might just as well have been eating sawdust for all the pleasure it gave her. Her appetite had long since disappeared and, as soon as she reasonably could, she would abandon the pretence of eating and leave.

She tried not to look across the room at Lawrence Cory, but couldn't resist the urge. In contrast to herself, he seemed to be absorbed in the enjoyment of his meal, oblivious to Kim's resentment and the growing interest of the two women who had taken note of his entrance earlier.

'I'm sure it's him,' one said in a carrying voice. 'He was there in the gallery the day I went.'

'Well, perhaps it is,' the other woman conceded, 'but, even if you're right, you can't just go up to him. . .'

'Why not?' The big woman stood up. 'He might find it flattering to be recognised.'

She crossed the dining-room, seemingly full of suppressed excitement.

Lawrence looked up as she approached him.

'I hope you don't mind,' she said with an ingratiating smile, 'but I just have to know. Are you Lawrence Cory?'

He frowned, as though he'd been dragged out of a deep reverie. 'Yes. That's right,' he answered on a note of obvious exasperation.

Kim wished she could pretend disinterest, but found she was straining her ears to listen.

'I knew it,' the woman squeaked with delight, and waved a hand to her friend. 'It is him. I told you so.'

People were beginning to take notice, and eyes turned in their direction as the other woman stood up excitedly and crossed to where Lawrence was sitting.

'Oh! This is so exciting!' she said. 'We thought your paintings were wonderful.'

'Wonderful,' the other repeated. She began to rummage in her cavernous bag. 'I still have the catalogue in here somewhere. Here it is.' She retrieved a crumpled booklet and held it aloft triumphantly. 'Do you think you could autograph it?'

A frown creased his forehead, giving him a dark, forbidding look that might have deterred a fainter heart.

'I'm not here to give autographs,' he said chillingly.

'Oh!' She looked crestfallen, but was obviously not to be put off that easily. Coaxingly, she held out the catalogue. 'Oh, do sign it, please. It would be such a thrill.'

Intrigued, in spite of herself, Kim watched as he took the proffered pen and signed hurriedly, waving away the women's thanks.

Joyfully, they began circulating the room with their prize, and the excitement grew. A number of people rose, obviously intending to make their way towards him.

He looked around with a kind of hunted expression on his face and his eyes met Kim's. Before she had time to look away, she saw the look of entreaty there, and the slight jerking movement of his head that begged for rescue. Almost before she knew what she was doing, she was on her feet, crossing to his table.

If she was expecting gratitude, she was disappointed. 'Sit down and try to look happy,' he hissed. 'I'll try not to make use of your services for too long.'

Two more women had arrived at the table, waving paper napkins.

'Do you think you could possibly——?'

Lawrence stood up.

'I'm sorry,' Kim heard him say, 'but my wife and I are just on our way out on to the terrace.' He grasped Kim's arm imperiously, bringing her awkwardly to her feet.

'My wife requests a little solitude.' He returned Kim's furiously indignant glare with a mocking twist of his lips, and his eyes gleamed with pure malice as he added, 'You know how it is, when you're on honeymoon.'

Meaningful smiles broke out on the faces of the autograph-seekers.

'We'll take our coffee on the terrace,' Lawrence told the waiter. 'If you could see that we're not disturbed?'

There was a momentary hush as they crossed the room, with Lawrence firmly holding Kim's elbow as they exited through the tall windows which led out on to the terrace, to be followed by a ripple of polite applause.

At first, Kim had been stunned by the unexpectedness of his mad declaration, but now she boiled with fury.

'How dare you?' she cried heatedly, as he steered

her to a table on the terrace, as far away as possible from the dining-room windows. 'You had no right to involve me in that fabrication.'

'I didn't ask. You offered,' he said unrepentantly, using her earlier remark outrageously against her.

'You did ask,' Kim argued hotly. 'I saw your eyes. They were desperate.'

'And you came to my rescue,' he gibed. 'How very touching.'

'And very stupid,' she gritted. 'I didn't expect to be dragged into a pack of lies.'

'Necessity is the mother of invention, my dear Miss Harris,' he said calmly. 'I know from experience that nothing will shake my fans loose once they've got their claws into me.'

'The perils of fame,' she pronounced sarcastically. 'Something you should be prepared to put up with.'

'I'm not that famous,' he said drily. 'It's just unfortunate that those two huntresses happened to be at one of the few gallery exhibitions I've had.'

To her annoyance, Kim felt faintly impressed. He was obviously quite a well-known artist. It added interest and a certain mystique, but didn't excuse his outrageous performance.

'You still had no right to bring me into it,' she said stubbornly. 'I'd like an apology.'

'Are you always so stuffy?' he asked casually. 'Don't you like basking in my reflected glory?'

'No, I am not. And no, I do not,' Kim spluttered, incensed by his conceit.

At that moment the waiter came with the coffee, and she sat back, simmering with silent indignation, as the man poured solicitously for them before leaving.

'It looks as though being on honeymoon turns people into invalids,' she said crabbily.

He laughed, the first sound of real amusement she'd heard from him.

'There you are! We're collecting the kudos already.' He pushed her cup towards her. 'Drink up. Then perhaps we'll take a little stroll.'

'You're very high-handed,' she cried irritably, adding, with intent and malice, 'for a hitch-hiker.'

'Ah! But that's only one of my facets,' he said easily.

Before she could stop herself, Kim answered bitingly, 'I believe that as a Gemini your facets are multi. I have noticed and, frankly, I'm surprised you don't get confused.'

'I sometimes do,' he replied evenly, a glimmer of mocking amusement in his amber eyes. 'I didn't realise you were into astrology.'

'I'm not,' Kim denied, angered at having given herself away. 'I just happened to be reading the paper.'

'I'm flattered you took the trouble to look me up.' His eyes narrowed challengingly. 'Having discovered one or two of my peculiar traits, aren't you intrigued to discover more?'

'Not in the slightest.' Kim's eyes were steely.

'You're a hard woman, Kimberley Harris,' he said ironically. 'But, just for now, be a good girl and drink up. I think the hordes are about to descend upon us again.'

Before she had a chance to comply or otherwise, the voices approaching grew louder, and he hauled her upright, almost lifting her off her feet with the speed he forced upon their exit.

The path they took led down into the pool area, where Lawrence Cory looked almost furtively around before depositing her at one of the small white tables on a balcony overlooking the gleaming water.

The night was dark, Kim noted, with only a thin

crescent moon and pinpoints of stars to brighten the sky. The pool's subdued lights added to the ethereal quality of the scene. The air was warm and the feather-light breeze caressed her.

Lawrence Cory leaned back in his seat with a sigh and closed his eyes. 'Peace at last.'

Despite herself, Kim began to see the funny side of the ridiculous episode. 'Was all this really necessary?'

He grinned at her and she saw the shadowy indentation in his cheek.

'Not entirely, perhaps,' he admitted, adding wickedly, 'but fun, don't you think?'

Kim felt some of the strange hostility draining away from her. Even she couldn't say why it had been so strong and why, at the moment, it seemed suddenly inappropriate.

She settled into her seat with a sigh that was almost contentment. 'Is that what you do for a living?' she asked quietly. 'Painting?'

'Yes,' he said after a pause. 'That among other things.'

She was tempted to ask what other things, but there was something beginning to gleam in the muted amber depths of his eyes that looked suspiciously like the kindling of deeper interest and she wondered if it was possible to backtrack a little without causing another quarrel.

But, before she could decide, he'd spoken.

'What about you? What do you do?'

Surprisingly, Kim felt none of the usual reluctance to talk about herself. 'I run my own engineering firm. It was my father's business until he died four years ago, and I've kept it going.'

He nodded. 'And you enjoyed it?'

Kim frowned. 'Of course. Why shouldn't I?'

He shrugged. 'Tough job, for a woman.'

'No tougher than for a man.' Kim felt the return of resentment. He had a positive talent for saying the wrong thing. 'You're not one of those men who think a woman's place is in the home, are you?'

'Not unless that's where she wants to be.'

His answer took the wind out of her sails and she flopped back into her chair with a tired sigh. 'Why is it we always seem to end up quarrelling?'

A smile curved the corner of his sensuous mouth.

'I don't know.' He leaned forward to take her hand in his. 'There are other things I'd far rather be doing.'

He brought her hand to his lips, their warm touch turning to fire against her fingers.

She tried unsuccessfully to snatch her hand away. 'I'm sure there are,' she said, annoyed to hear the huskiness in her voice. 'Unfortunately for you, I'm not of the same mind.'

'Aren't you?'

He rose and drew her to her feet, still holding her hand.

He began to draw her into his arms.

'Let go, please,' she said, her voice ragged with a hint of rising panic.

He released her immediately.

'If you don't mind,' she said jerkily, 'I'm tired. I'd like to go to bed.'

She moved nervously to one side as he seemed to block her way. She'd been a fool to think they could be friends.

'Don't go. Talk with me a little while longer. Let's see if we can't find a way over this barrier that seems always to be between us.'

'I don't know what you mean.' Kim avoided his searching eyes. 'Let me pass.'

He held up his hand in a gesture of acknowledgement. 'Look, I'm sorry if I overstepped some invisible mark. I didn't mean to frighten you.'

Kim bit her lip, embarrassed that he'd seen that flash of near panic. 'You didn't. I'm just tired. It's been a long, tiring day.'

'So it has. But I have a feeling there's something other than that bothering you.'

'There's nothing bothering me,' Kim denied, feeling suddenly shaky. He was getting too close again. 'Please! There's no point to this.'

He grasped her arms urgently. 'There's every point,' he insisted. 'I hate unsolved riddles.'

'There's no riddle to solve,' she said tensely, feeling the fiery shock of his touch. 'I just want to be left alone.'

'I know.' His grip tightened, drawing her nearer. 'What I don't yet know is why.'

'No reason,' she denied, her temper flaring. 'Except an aversion to conceited, predatory males.'

He made an impatient sound. 'Is that really how I come across? Or are we talking about somebody else?'

He caught her chin with his free hand, forcing her eyes up to his. 'Who was he, Kim?'

His face was shadowed in the dim light of the moon, but his eyes gleamed with an almost mesmeric intensity. 'He'd have to hurt you very badly to cause this much shut-down.'

'I. . . I don't know what you're talking about,' she lied shakily.

'Then what are you afraid of?' he asked, his voice soft, almost sensual. 'Not of me, surely?'

'I'm not afraid of anything.'

He moved so that his back was against the rail, his broad outline silhouetted against the faint moonlight, suddenly mysterious. He turned Kim, so that her face was out of the shadows.

'Not even yourself?' His gaze probed mercilessly into her widened eyes.

'Don't be ridiculous,' she scoffed, holding his gaze coldly. 'Why should I be afraid of myself?'

He laughed softly. 'Only you know the answer to that.'

Kim made a short exasperated sound. 'If this is another of your games. . . I'm afraid I'm not in the mood.'

She tugged to free her hand, but he held on. 'Let go of me.' She was trembling visibly. 'Please!'

He sighed deeply and released her. 'At this point, I could be tempted to give up.'

'I wish you would,' Kim cut in with a return of spirit, 'because you're wasting your time.'

He lifted a surprisingly gentle hand to caress her cheek.

Kim pulled back as the powerful charge of his vitality exploded through her body. 'As I told you before. . .' her voice was ragged '. . .I'm not interested.'

He smiled. 'Do you know your pupils dilate when you tell a lie?'

Kim lowered her lids quickly and turned away. 'A trick of the moon, Mr Cory,' she said quellingly. 'The moon is said to govern delusions.'

'So I've heard.' She felt his touch briefly on her hair. 'But who is deluding whom?'

His hands rested lightly on her shoulders as he moved past her and then turned so that he was once again facing her.

Kim stiffened, awaiting whatever was to happen next.

His head dipped suddenly and his mouth captured

hers in a gentle kiss. The sweet pressure of his lips seemed to be drawing her very soul out of her body and Kim felt a shudder begin deep inside her. If it rose, it would engulf her.

Somehow, she managed to pull back.

'How many times do I have to tell you?' she said shakily. 'I don't want you. . .'

He put a finger to her lips. 'That's all right,' he said softly. 'I'll wait until you do.'

Kim's breath seemed to be squeezed out of her body by a giant hand.

'Goodnight, Miss Harris,' he murmured, with a little smile. 'Sweet dreams.'

But she'd slept restlessly, and woke with dark circles beneath her eyes. She got up immediately and showered, packing away the few things she had brought out of her case the night before. She was downstairs, ready to leave, just before six o'clock.

Monsieur Dubois was there behind his desk, looking as spruce and neat as always. Kim wondered absently if he ever slept.

'Could I have my bill, please?'

He presented her with his meticulous invoice, accepting payment with a shake of his head.

'You don't wish to have breakfast, *mademoiselle*?' The little hotelier looked scandalised. 'It is only six o'clock and the kitchen is not yet open, but it would be no trouble for me to make some for you.'

Kim shook her head.

He was a kind man and it obviously distressed him to send a guest away unfed, but she was in a hurry.

'I want to make an early start to beat the traffic,' she explained, only half truthfully. 'I can always pick up some food on the way.'

It would have to be at a *pâtisserie* in some little French village along the way, she decided determinedly. There would be no more unscheduled stops at motorway services.

Outside, the air was already warm, and the sky was clear and bright with the promise of a lovely day.

Her car was already around the front of the hotel and her boot was open. How kind of Monsieur Dubois to anticipate her needs. He had sent a sleepy Henri up to collect her cases as she paid her bill. He was coming down the steps now.

'Good morning. Looks like the rain's gone for good.'

Kim started and stared at the tall figure carrying her cases. 'Oh, no!' she breathed.

'Did you sleep well?' Lawrence Cory's amber eyes scanned her face, which she knew was pale and shadowed.

'Not particularly,' she said tightly. 'Did you sleep *at all*?'

'Like a log. But I always wake early.' He stored her cases in the boot and tossed his own bag in beside them. 'If you're tired,' he said amicably, 'I could always do the driving.'

Kim gritted her teeth. 'I don't remember offering you another lift.'

He stood looking at her, his hand on the open lid of the boot. He was wearing light trousers with a close-fitting T-shirt which followed the contours of his muscular chest and shoulders and Kim couldn't restrain the sharp intake of her breath.

His sharp eyes probed hers with a hint of amused understanding. 'I hope you're not getting a cold, after yesterday's soaking.'

'No. The choking noise you hear is indignation,' Kim said tartly. 'I got up especially early to avoid you.'

'I thought you might,' he said sardonically. 'Do you mean my company is not welcome?'

She nodded grimly. 'That's what I mean.'

His brows drew together in a frown. 'You won't reconsider?' He spread his hands. 'Not even if I promise not to psychoanalyse you?'

'Not even then.'

His eyes probed hers, but she kept them steady. This time it was she who had to win.

Recognising the unswerving hardness of her resolve, he seemed suddenly to give up.

'Oh, well. It's back to the thumb.' He frowned consideringly. 'Do you think it would help if I rolled up my trouser-leg?'

Kim steadfastly refused to smile. This light facetiousness was unfamiliar. No doubt one of the facets he'd invited her to explore, she thought drily.

'Perhaps. . .who knows?' she answered him in the same vein. 'Perhaps one of your fans will oblige.'

She had a sneaky feeling she was hitting below the belt, but was incapable of caring. All she wanted was to get away. . .fast.

'Now, if you wouldn't mind removing that.' She indicated his bag with an imperious hand.

With a shrug, he hooked his bag out of the boot and slammed the lid. 'You're making a mistake,' he said. 'There's a lot of truth in the old adage—better the devil you know than the one you don't.'

'Don't worry,' she said implacably. 'I won't be giving a lift to any more devils.'

She got into the car, arranged herself comfortably and shut the door with a snap.

He was standing by, watching her, but she refused to meet his eyes. 'Goodbye!' she said, with an air of finality.

He waved silently, a thin smile curving his lips.

Kim drove purposefully off but, despite her resolve, risked a glance in the rear-view mirror. He was already walking back to the hotel.

CHAPTER THREE

'KIM!'

The front door opened and Pam's small figure came hurtling down the path. 'You've arrived at last. I was beginning to wonder if you'd got lost.'

Kim laughed. 'Once or twice I almost did.'

Pam enveloped Kim in an extravagant hug and, with an arm around her shoulders, almost dragged her towards the house.

'Come on in! I've loads to tell you.'

Kim sighed. 'And I was hoping for a restful evening,' she joked.

Pam grinned. 'Well, if you're that tired, I'll have to wait until tomorrow.'

'Thoughtful of you,' Kim quipped. 'Being in love has already made a new woman of you. I wonder if Georges realises the miracle?'

Pam's face glowed.

'Oh, Georges! He's a miracle in himself, and I still can't believe my luck.'

Kim felt a small twinge of envy, hastily smothered. With Pam looking so radiantly happy, it would be worth her own pain.

Pam ushered her into the small hall.

'Is the miracle about?' Kim looked around, feeling a little apprehensive at the thought of meeting Pam's paragon.

'No. He's helping his mother sort out the sleeping arrangements for those of his friends and relatives who have travelled long-distance.' She pulled a little face.

'A nuisance, but I'll have him all to myself in a couple of days, so I can't really complain.'

She led Kim into the low-ceilinged living-room. 'Besides, it gives us a chance to have a little get-together of our own.' She indicated the sofa. 'Make yourself comfortable while I get you some coffee. . .or would you prefer tea?'

Kim sank down gratefully and stretched her legs out before her. 'A cup of tea would be heaven,' she said.

Pam brought the tray in and put it on a coffee-table close to the sofa. 'How was your trip down?' she asked as she poured Kim's tea.

'Fine.'

'Did you meet anyone *interesting* on the way?'

Kim hid a smile.

Pam was always trying to put her in the way of *interesting* men. The trouble was, Pam's idea of interesting didn't always coincide with Kim's.

'No. No one the smallest bit interesting.'

Kim watched as Pam's face fell and wondered how she would react if she told her about Lawrence Cory. She'd probably never hear the end of the subject.

Later, after they'd eaten, Pam set light to the logs in the grate and switched on the table lamps.

'It doesn't really get cold here at this time of year, but it's so much cosier with a fire, don't you think?'

Kim looked wonderingly at her friend's glowing face. 'You're really at home here, aren't you, Pam?'

Pam sank down into the armchair opposite and for once her mobile features were serene. 'Home is the word,' she said. 'It's the first real home I've had.' She waved her hand expressively. 'I don't mean this cottage—obviously it's not mine and it's not permanent—but this place. . .these people. . . They're mine.'

Kim bit her lip.

Pam had lost her parents at a young age and had been brought up by her mother's unmarried sister, who'd done her best for her young niece. Moneywise, Pam had been more than comfortably provided for, but in terms of family life she hadn't been so lucky.

Her aunt had had her own career to pursue and having a young child to care for had been inconvenient. Pam had gone to boarding-school at the age of ten and, from choice, had lived alone since she was eighteen.

She hadn't *had* to work to live, and had drifted in and out of one job after another. . .one romance after another. . .

'I know you think I'm mad,' Pam went on a little defensively, 'rushing into marriage this way. But it's all so right for me.' Her eyes turned misty. 'Coming here. . .meeting Georges was meant to be. . .it was my destiny.'

Kim shook her head. 'I don't think you're mad,' she said softly. 'I just worry about you.'

Pam reached across to squeeze her hand. 'I know. But from now on you needn't.'

She sat back and sighed. 'After Saturday, I'll be practically out of your life. I've got my future all sorted out, so now it's my turn to worry about you. It's one thing to bury yourself in that mouldy old business of yours, but one day, when you're middle-aged and still sitting behind that desk of yours, you'll wonder where your life went.'

Kim laughed uneasily. 'Just because I run my own business doesn't mean I can't manage a relationship, a marriage. . .'

Pam snorted inelegantly. 'Oh, you might manage one all right. With a cold fish like Charles. . .*manage* would probably be the right word.'

Kim frowned. 'I didn't say I was going to marry Charles.'

'No.' Pam agreed. 'But you probably will.'

Kim bit her lip and looked away from Pam's discerning eyes. 'I haven't made up my mind yet, but. . .probably.'

Pam stood up and began pacing agitatedly up and down. 'Over my dead body!' she cried vehemently. 'You're worth more than a token marriage.'

Kim stiffened. 'It wouldn't be a token marriage. And Charles isn't a cold fish. He's a kind, dependable man who would always be there when I need him.'

'But it's not him you *need*,' Pam insisted. 'You need a man who can stimulate you; make you laugh, make you cry. . .transport you out of that cool, critical, Virgo mind of yours.'

For some reason, Lawrence Cory's face rose strongly into Kim's mind's eye, filling her with a peculiar emptiness. . .sand slipping inexorably through her fingers. . . She pushed the vision away.

'I'll bear all those criteria in mind if I ever really do choose a husband,' she said lightly.

But, for once, Pamela was determinedly serious. She stood up and went to stand at the window, looking out at the clear starry sky. 'I'm scatty. I know that,' she said jerkily. 'Impulsive. . .unpredictable. . .' She turned to face Kim, her hands clenched tightly. 'But at least I know how to listen to my heart.'

She shook her head impatiently. 'Do you think I haven't watched you giving the cold shoulder to every half-decent-looking man who was foolish enough to come within freezing distance of you?' She spread her hands in a helpless gesture. 'You're so typically stuffy sometimes, I could hit you, but you're not made of ice. For heaven's sake, let the real Kimberley Harris out. . .give her a chance. And, more importantly, give someone else a chance to get close to you. . .'

Kim stared at Pam, her heart beating unevenly.

'Not made of ice'. The words echoed in her head. 'Ice-woman', Philip had labelled her. 'No woman at all. . .frigid. . .'

Pam had been her friend for a long time, but not even she knew the full humiliation of her broken love-affair.

Kim bit hard on her lower lip to stop its sudden trembling.

'I don't know how much being a Virgo has to do with anything,' she said musingly. 'Precious little, I suspect. Perhaps the real explanation is that I've never met any man even remotely worth the chance.'

Pam—this new, confident, almost maternal Pam—came and put her arms about her shoulders. 'But you will one day, I know it.'

'I wish I had your optimism,' Kim said, feeling suddenly drained. She rubbed her hand across her forehead.

'Oh, lord!' Pam exclaimed. 'Now I've upset you.'

'No, you haven't.' Kim smiled at Pam's melodrama, despite herself. 'I'm just tired.'

Pam's uncharacteristically troubled brown eyes met hers. 'Are you sure there's nothing wrong?'

Kim gave herself a little mental shake. 'Nothing a good night's sleep won't cure.'

But sleep cured nothing. She dreamed of mazes out of which she could find no exit. . .and of huge chunks of ice which followed around behind her, threatening to overtake and flatten her if she should dare pause in her search for an escape. . .

* * *

The sound of the telephone penetrated Kim's exhausting and disturbed sleep. As it continued to ring, she groaned and rolled on to her side, letting her mind come awake. Who on earth could it be? And where was Pam?

She sat up groggily and pushed back the bedclothes, swinging her legs over the side of the bed, her toes blindly searching for her slippers.

The telephone stopped as she was shrugging into her robe.

'Damn!' she growled. Now she would be left to wonder who had been ringing and whether it was important. If it was important, she reasoned irritably, then the person would be certain to ring back.

She was tempted to go back to bed, but decided against it. It had been nearly dawn before she'd settled into undisturbed slumber; her head felt heavy and numb, and she was desperate for a cup of tea.

She would go downstairs and make a pot and, if Pam was still in bed, she would take her up a cup.

But Pam was in the hall as Kim went down the steep narrow stairs and she looked as though she'd been up for hours.

'Did you get the telephone?' Kim asked sleepily.

'Only just. I was out in the garden when it started ringing. Do you want any breakfast?'

'Just a cup of tea,' Kim said, following her into the kitchen. 'But if you twist my arm, I might manage a slice of toast.'

'Coming up.' Pam slipped two pieces of bread into the toaster. 'That was Estelle, Georges's mother. She wants me to go over to the house later.'

She poured a mug of tea from the pot and pushed it across the table to Kim.

Kim took it and drank thirstily, before answering,

'Well, that's OK. You go. There's no need to worry about me.'

Pam grimaced. 'I won't be worrying about you. I'll be too busy worrying about myself. Georges's family are gathering from far and wide and his mother has planned a get-together this evening for the female members of the clan.' She groaned. 'There are dozens of them, Kim, most of whom I haven't met, and I'm terrified. What if they hate me?'

Kim laughed. 'I shouldn't worry too much. I'm sure that once they've got over the shock they'll like you well enough.'

'Oh, please! Don't tease!' Pam wailed. 'I'm serious.'

'They won't hate you, you idiot,' Kim assured her, startled by the uncharacteristic note of panic in Pam's voice. 'Calm down.'

'It wouldn't be so bad if Georges was going to be there,' Pam went on crossly. 'But he's spending the evening with his friends and relatives, male of course, and they'll probably be having a whale of a time.'

'It is traditional,' Kim reminded her amusedly. 'Even in France, I gather.'

Absently, she took the piece of toast Pam handed her and spread it with butter.

'Your female get-together probably won't be as bad as you imagine,' she said comfortingly. 'What time will you be going?'

'We,' Pam corrected her. 'What time will *we* be going? You've got to come. I need your moral support.'

'Must I?' Kim sighed. 'I was rather hoping I'd have a little peace and quiet to lie around in the sun.'

'You'll have plenty of time for lying around in the sun when I'm married and have gone on my honey-moon,' Pam said firmly, and then added coaxingly,

'Oh, please, Kim! I've got to have somebody on my side.'

'You make it sound more like a war than a wedding,' Kim said sardonically. 'But since you can't do without me, I suppose I'll have to go.'

'Wonderful!' Pam hooted in triumph. 'Georges will be here at about four o'clock.' Her eyes took on that bright glow. 'You'll love him when you see him. But remember, he's mine.'

'As if I'd dare forget.'

Georges was every bit as nice as Pam had said. He had dark hair which was a little wild, an olive-skinned, open face and a wide smile, which reached right up to his warm brown eyes. Though shorter than Kim had anticipated, he still managed to stand head and shoulders over Pam. And her friend needn't have worried, Kim thought wryly. Georges only had eyes for his bride.

Kim felt a sense of relief. It looked as though this time Pam had got it right, after all.

'This is Georges,' Pam said, her face glowing with pride. 'And this, my darling Georges, is my very closest friend, Kimberley Harris.'

'*Enchanté*.'

He kissed Kim on both cheeks and for a moment, as he met her appraising glance, his smile faded a little, to be replaced by a look of anxiety. He was obviously every bit as worried about meeting her as Pam was about meeting his family.

Kim gave him a wide smile. 'I'm so happy to meet you at last,' she said.

He relaxed at her friendly tone and his wide grin returned. 'Pamela has told me so much about you,' he said in halting English that added to his charm.

'Is that why you were looking so terrified?' she joked. 'Whatever Pam may say, I don't really gobble men up for breakfast.'

'*Mon Dieu!* I hope not,' he said gravely, and they all laughed.

Kim sat in the back of the car, almost speechless with surprise as they turned in at tall, elaborate stone gates. When Kim had told her Georges's family had a vineyard, she hadn't imagined for one moment the extent of it. The land stretched for miles in every direction, and the house, when they arrived, was almost a mansion.

'You're going to live here?' she said incredulously to Pam as they stepped out of the car.

'Not here.' Pam laughed at the awe on Kim's face. 'Georges's parents have given us a smaller place as a wedding-present. Our house, with its own vineyard, is about ten miles from here. It's being renovated at the moment and won't be ready until we come back from our honeymoon in a month's time. Georges's friend is drawing up the plans and supervising the work. I can't wait to see the finished result.'

She tucked her hand through Kim's arm as they walked together towards the house, and Georges drove the car around the back.

'I won't be needing the cottage after tomorrow, so you can stay there as long as you want, provided it's not more than the seven weeks left on the letting. After that, it's up for sale.'

Kim laughed. 'I shan't be needing it for anything like seven weeks. A week or ten days is the most I can spare away from the office.'

'That damned office!' Pam frowned. 'What you really need is a wonderful man to sweep you off your feet, so that you don't care if you never go back there.' She shot Kim a sly look. 'I suppose ten days is better than nothing.'

A trickle of apprehension ran down Kim's back. 'Pam. If you've got any ideas, I'll——'

'How could I have?' She looked innocently up at the sky. 'Eligible men aren't that thick on the ground around these parts.'

'I'm relieved to hear it,' Kim said sardonically.

'But I was just thinking. Georges's friend, the one who's doing the renovations, is an architect, and he's thinking of buying a business in the town close by here. I haven't actually met him yet, but from his voice on the phone he sounds absolutely gorgeous.' She hugged Kim's arm tightly with a look of joyous anticipation on her face. 'Just think. If you married him and came to live here, perhaps bought Mill Cottage—that's what its French name means—we'd be practically neighbours, and I wouldn't be homesick with you around, and you'd have something else to think about other than that damned business of yours.'

She paused for breath.

'Wouldn't that be wonderful?'

'And wouldn't it be wonderful if life was that simple?' Kim laughed. 'I don't suppose it occurs to you that this architect friend of Georges's could have plans for his own future, which do not include marrying a woman he's never even met? Or perhaps he already has a woman in mind for that honour.'

'Oh, but he hasn't,' Pam insisted seriously. 'He's free and he's available, and if you would only relax and be yourself when you meet him he'll be bound to fall for you.'

Kim came to an abrupt halt, disentangled her arm, and caught Pam by the shoulders, turning her, none too gently, to face her. 'Pamela Brown! What do you mean, *when* I meet him? If you're up to your old tricks of setting me up, I'll. . . I'll. . .'

She stopped, searching her mind for the worst torture she could inflict.

'Don't be silly,' Pam said hastily. 'I haven't set anything up. He'll be at the wedding, so you're bound to meet him. How do you know it won't be love at first sight?'

'Pam,' Kim cut in, horrified. 'If you dare to embarrass me by even hinting to Georges's friend about any of this nonsense, I swear I'll never speak to you again.'

'Oh, for heaven's sake!' Pam said with a resigned sigh. 'Why do you always have to be so stuffy? I only want what's best for you.'

'Not to mention what's best for you,' Kim replied grimly. 'I think I'll be the judge of what's best for me. . .and I want you to promise——'

'OK. . .OK. . .' Pam broke in hurriedly. 'I promise.' She gave an exaggerated sigh. 'There! Now are you satisfied?'

'I wish I could be absolutely sure I was,' Kim said with a frown.

'This is Kimberley Harris, Pamela's friend from England.'

Kim smiled, but hid a silent groan. She was getting a little tired of hearing this repeated every dozen steps or so.

Estelle Baron was leading Kim about the room, her hand lightly against her elbow, introducing her to the surprisingly large number of women who had gathered in the big airy drawing-room.

A tall willowy brunette took Kim's hand and shook it delicately.

'This is Simone,' Estelle explained, gently pinching

the girl's cheek. 'She's my brother's daughter and my favourite niece.'

Simone smiled at her aunt and kissed her, but the look she turned on Kim, through green, slightly upslanting eyes, was less than cordial.

'I am so glad Pamela had found *someone* to invite to the wedding after all,' she said, her voice attractively husky, despite the obvious barb.

Kim's blue eyes narrowed. 'Yes,' she agreed evenly. 'Pam and I are like sisters, having both lost our parents. Not everyone has a family like yours, Simone. You're very fortunate.'

'I am indeed.' The green eyes glittered. 'As is your friend Pamela. . .to have won our hearts.'

'Indeed. Indeed.' Estelle urged Kim on.

'Simone is a good girl,' Estelle said by way of explanation, 'but a little possessive.'

And a malicious troublemaker, Kim added silently. Given the chance. Hopefully, Pam wouldn't be seeing too much of Cousin Simone, Kim thought, mentally crossing her fingers, though it was difficult to see how she could spoil things between Pam and Georges.

They continued working their way around the room to greet even more new arrivals. Could they all be relatives? Kim wondered in awe.

Estelle laughed, correctly interpreting Kim's expression. 'Fortunately, it isn't often the whole family gathers in this way,' she said. '*C'est formidable, non?*'

'Yes,' Kim answered. 'To be honest, my head is beginning to spin a little. When we've finished the introductions, I think I'd like some fresh air.'

'Ah! We finish now.' Estelle made a soft tutting sound. 'How thoughtless I am.' She ushered Kim towards the tall french windows. 'Go into the garden and I will bring you a drink and a little something to eat.'

'Oh, no! Don't put yourself to that trouble,' Kim protested. 'I'll get something from the buffet myself before I go outside.'

'Are you sure?' Estelle was obviously torn between good manners and the other duties of a hostess. Hands were waving in her direction.

'Perfectly sure.'

Pam hadn't really been in need of her moral support after all, and Kim had been left alone in a sea of strangers until Estelle Baron had kindly come to her rescue.

The bride-to-be had been besieged the moment they'd stepped through the doorway. She'd looked apologetically over her shoulder at Kim before being whisked away, but was now the centre of attention of an excited, laughing group and apparently oblivious to Kim's presence.

She thought about the buffet, but her stomach was in a knot of nerves and it was unlikely that she would be able to swallow a bite. What she really needed was some fresh air, she decided, and she made her way towards the tall french windows which were open to the garden.

Kim slipped, unnoticed, from the room. Once outside, she took a deep breath of the blossom-scented air and exhaled on a sigh.

It was a beautiful garden, its wide sweep of lawn bordered by masses of flowers and with little tree-shaded arbours placed discreetly around the tiered stone terraces.

The place was empty for the moment. Seemingly, every guest—all female—was crammed into the large drawing-room, each one apparently unwilling to miss a moment of the exciting lead-up to the wedding.

Georges had disappeared shortly after they'd arrived. His father had stayed on to greet some of the first arrivals, but after about half an hour he too had slipped discreetly away.

Kim wandered freely along the stone pathways, with no sense of time or direction, until she came upon a stand of tall cedars which marked the eastern boundary of the grounds. There was a weathered wooden fence with a stile, and Kim clambered over it into a field which was covered with yellow flowers, reaching almost waist high, their brightness outshining even the sun. Red poppies interspersed the yellow carpet with flashes of crimson and Kim gave in to the urge to sit down in the midst of all this wonderful colour to take a rest.

The sun bore down on her head, making her drowsy. After her restless night, Kim was overpowered by the urge to lie down and close her eyes. She did so with a sigh of contentment, and stretched out comfortably.

She was woken by the sound of a whistle, too tuneless to be a bird, and opened heavy eyelids, which she hastily shaded against the sun's bright rays.

For an instant, she thought she was hallucinating.

A man was sitting a short distance away with his legs crossed and a sketch-book resting on his knees. His dark head was bent with concentration as he guided his pencil over the paper, a light whistle sounding thinly through his teeth.

Kim closed and opened her eyes a number of times before she could believe their evidence.

'You!' she cried accusingly, when she could trust herself to speak. 'I thought I was still dreaming.'

Without lifting his head, or pausing in his sketching, he said, 'Have you been dreaming of me, then?'

Kim drew in a sharp breath. More than once, as she'd lain on the verge of sleep, her mind had surfaced into consciousness, shocked by the awareness that she had been lying in Lawrence Cory's arms. . .her body, scorched by the heat of him, melting away into nothingness. . .a sun-induced daydream of guilty frustration. . .

'What are you doing here?' she asked a little raggedly.

'I should have thought that was obvious. I'm sketching.'

'Sketching what?' she demanded, and then sat up at the sudden realisation. 'Sketching me? Without asking? How dare you?'

'You were sleeping,' he answered reasonably, still without raising his head or stilling the movement of his pencil. 'So I could hardly ask. Besides, I wanted to sketch you asleep, like a tousled child, freed from that hurt "touch me not" mask you like to wear.'

'You've no right!' she cried, angrily aware that his remark hurt far more than it should.

She straightened her dress and leaned forward furiously to snatch the sketch-block from his hands, hardly daring to look at it for fear of what it might reveal. The same fear drove her to look.

Only one side of her face, only the forward edge of the angle of her body, had been sketched in. . .and yet it conveyed, with appalling vividness, the feeling of awful emptiness which had pervaded her for weeks.

'That isn't me,' she denied sickly.

'It isn't finished,' he said with an irritable sigh. 'And I'd be glad if you never did that again. I have a strong aversion to anyone's seeing an unfinished piece of my work.'

'It's never going to be finished.' Her fingers felt thick

and unwieldy as she strove to tear the sheet from the block.

Before she could even take a firm hold, his hand clamped about her wrist like steel. 'Don't.' The one word fell like granite, shocking her, by its harshness, into immobility.

He wrenched the block from her and set it aside as he continued to imprison her wrist in his cruel grasp. 'Aren't you even going to say hello?'

He was mocking her, Kim knew, the steely glint in his eye muting to gleaming cynicism.

'Hello,' she said defiantly. 'Does that make you happy? Now let go of me.'

His hold relaxed a little to become almost a caress as his thumb moved gently against the soft underside of her wrist. 'A little. I might be happier if you said you were pleased to see me.' His mouth curled at one corner. 'But I won't ask the impossible.'

He released her hand and tore the top sheet off his block. 'Since you want this so much, I'll make a gift of it to you.'

Kim's breast was still heaving with anger and the pain of his rough hold on her. 'Thank you. Since it's mine, I trust I can now do as I please with it?'

He nodded, his eyes narrowed on her. 'Of course.'

'Thank you.' Hardly knowing why she felt so vindictive, she tore it into pieces and threw it towards him. 'I'm sure you can do better than that.'

'Oh! I'm sure I can.'

Without warning, he reached forward and grabbed her wrists, jerking her towards him so forcefully that she lay full length on the ground beside him. As she began to struggle, he put his leg across hers, pinning her with his weight and holding her wrists above her head. His face was close to hers, so that she could smell the clean tangy scent of his skin, feel the warmth of his breath, see the flame of anger burning in his amber eyes.

'Though why I should want to bother with a spiteful, self-centred little——'

Suddenly his head dipped, bringing his mouth down to cover her lips roughly, bruising their unprepared softness, sending spearheads of unidentifiable sensation coursing through her.

Stubbornly, grimly, she fought him.

Caught at the wrists, pinned by his weight, she could only writhe in frustrated fury.

'Stay still, you little fool,' he lifted his lips to murmur raggedly. 'I'm not made of stone.'

'Then let me go.' Her voice was a hoarse angry whisper.

'Not until you relax and kiss me back.'

'I don't want to kiss you.' She resumed her struggles, her body thrusting hard against his in an attempt to lift his leg from hers, collapsing, breathless, as her strength ebbed.

His lips brushed tantalisingly against hers. 'Wasn't that nice?' he murmured enticingly. 'Why do we always have to fight?'

His bright eyes mocked her, his mouth curved tormentingly only inches from her own. 'If you'd only let the barriers down, there's no telling what else you might enjoy.'

Kim gasped, her breath hissing inwards sharply through her teeth.

'And if I don't enjoy it—what then?' she challenged him with a glare.

He frowned in exasperation. 'Well, I certainly wouldn't force you. It's not my style.'

'If you mean it, let me go.'

He smiled into her half-frightened, half-indignant face. 'I do mean it.' He kissed the tip of her nose, briefly, teasingly. 'Gentle persuasion is more in my line.'

He relaxed his hold a little, lightening his weight, so that Kim was able to take a deep breath.

He was going to let her go. . .release her from the strange pressure that was building up inside.

But his mouth was on hers again, this time softly demanding, the unexpected movement against her lips startling her into a reluctant response, which grew as his kiss deepened and became exploring, sweet, stirring something exquisitely painful within her. His right hand released its hold on her wrist and moved caressingly down her arm, across her breast, following the sweep of her waist, drawing her hips closer to his taut body, making her aware of his heated arousal.

Involuntarily her own body arched to him and her arm came down to hook about his neck.

With a little sighing sound, he released her other arm and drew her urgently against him.

'Ice-woman,' Philip had labelled her, she remembered in the erratic jumble of her thoughts. So why was she being slowly consumed by a fire which rose uncontrollably from within her own trembling body?

'Is this a private party, or can anyone join in?' The cool light voice spoke in charmingly accented English.

Kim's eyes flew open, breaking the spell which had threatened to overpower her senses.

As Lawrence lifted his head, Kim found herself staring up into Simone's amused and faintly contemptuous face.

'Remarkable,' the girl said. 'I always thought you English so cold and reserved.' She laughed lightly. 'I must remember to warn my dear cousin Georges to keep a close eye on his little English miss.'

Her eyes swept over Lawrence, who was lying propped on one elbow, calmly surveying her in turn.

'However, I can understand your temptation, *ma chérie*.' With another laugh, she turned lightly on her heel and left them.

Kim buried her burning face in her arms. 'I'll never forgive you,' she said, her voice low and venomous. 'Never.' She shuddered. 'I have never been so humiliated.'

'That's a lot of *nevers*.' He was laughing, touching her shoulder, trying to turn her to face him.

'And that girl. . .of all people. . .' Kim groaned. 'She obviously thinks. . .' She drew to a halt, shrugging his hand away.

'And she was right,' he cut in drily. 'You were enjoying being made love to, making love in return. Is that so terrible?'

'I wasn't enjoying it.' Kim scrambled to her feet. 'You took me by surprise.'

'Did I?' He got up and stood looking down into her flushed angry face. 'Perhaps that's the best way to get through to you,' he said, his gaze holding hers narrowly, unrepentant. 'I must remember that for the future.'

'There isn't any future!' Kim blazed, her chin set stubbornly. 'I never want to see you again.'

'Well, you'd better keep your eyes closed all day tomorrow.' He grinned. 'I'm best man at Georges's wedding.'

CHAPTER FOUR

'LAWRENCE CORY,' Kim said, and Pamela looked up in surprise.

They were back at the cottage, sitting together cross-legged on the fireside rug, sipping at cups of hot chocolate.

'Lawrence Cory,' Pam repeated. 'I didn't know you knew him.'

'I think you know I do.'

Kimberley gave a silent sigh. She hadn't meant to raise this now, not wanting to risk an upset with Pam so near to the wedding, but it had been eating away at her for the whole evening. Simone's hostile, challenging stares, following her about the crowded room, hadn't helped her temper, but she'd resisted the urge to rise to the bait.

'What do you mean?' Pam frowned in puzzlement.

Kim laughed, a surprisingly harsh sound. 'Didn't you put him on to me?' she accused. 'It can hardly have been coincidence that he spotted me on the ferry and then latched on to me virtually the whole way down.'

Pamela's astonishment seemed incredibly real, Kim noted sourly, as her friend's mouth dropped open.

'Did he?' she queried. 'But you told me you didn't meet anybody interesting on the way over, so how was I to know he'd found you?'

'Ah ha!' Kim cried triumphantly. 'So you did set me up.'

'No. Of course I didn't.' Pam's face was flushed with indignation. 'I spoke to him on the telephone last week, when he rang Georges to say he would be travelling over by car with two of his friends. I did mention my friend was coming over at the same time. I asked him to keep an eye out for you and to introduce himself if he got the opportunity. I told him roughly what you looked like and hoped you'd meet up. What's wrong with that?'

Without giving Kim a chance to answer, she rushed on. 'I thought you'd feel less of an outsider if you knew at least one of the other guests in advance. I was only thinking of you.'

'Again,' Kim added grimly.

So he hadn't actually been hitching, she thought furiously. Why then had he pretended that he was? The two people he was with at the motorway services had apparently been the friends he'd planned to travel with. Why had he let them go on without him, instead of getting them to wait for him when he'd stopped to change her wheel? The answer seemed obvious.

'He's the architect you were talking about earlier on, isn't he?' she said accusingly. 'The one you already had me married to in your mind. Don't tell me that wasn't the idea.'

Pam drained the last of her hot chocolate and put the mug down in the hearth. 'Well, what if it was?'

She turned her unrepentant gaze on Kim.

'As I said earlier, I don't want you turning into an old maid because of a man like Philip Crossley.'

'If I do, it will be from my own choice,' Kim said sharply and then, as a thought occurred to her, she felt the colour drain from her face. 'You didn't tell him about Philip, did you?'

'Of course not,' Pam said derisively. 'I wouldn't want him to think you were stupid enough to be still mooning about a love-affair that went wrong years ago.'

Kim let out her pent-up breath in a sigh. Thank heavens she had never confided the whole wretched story to Pam. It was obvious that she would have had no conscience about using the knowledge to further her aim of finding Kim a man.

'I am not mooning about anybody,' Kim said firmly. 'And I'd be grateful if you'd keep your long nose out of my affairs in future. Remember, you promised.'

Pam turned irritably away. 'All right.' She lifted her hands in a dramatic gesture of defeat. 'I give up. If you want to miss out on love, it's up to you.'

'Thank you.' Kim pulled her mouth into a straight line. 'I'd rather that than be made love to by a man who was put up to it by my scheming *best* friend. What did you do, Pam? Ask him to give me a crash course in lovemaking?'

Pam sat bolt upright, a look of unholy glee on her face. 'He made love to you?'

Kim snorted inelegantly. 'I'd call it assault. The man's a menace. Arrogant. . .conceited. . .overbearing.'

Pam laughed delightedly. 'I haven't even met him yet, but he sounds wonderful.'

'You would think so.'

Pam giggled. 'Is he good-looking?' she asked in a confiding tone that irritated Kim.

'He thinks he is,' she said nastily.

Not strictly true, she amended silently; he wasn't so much conceited as supremely confident. In anyone else, she conceded, such confidence might be attractive, but in Lawrence Cory it aroused only intense irritation.

'Where and when did he make love to you?' Pam asked, suspiciously casual.

'He didn't,' Kim said, wishing she hadn't let her tongue run away with her. 'He just tried.'

And she'd helped him; she couldn't deny to herself her own responsive part in the stupid incident. If Simone hadn't come along when she did. . .Her toes curled in embarrassment at the picture she must have presented to the French girl, lying half beneath a man who was almost a stranger, returning kiss for kiss. . .

'If you don't mind, I'd rather not discuss it.' Kim had some satisfaction from seeing the look of disappointment on Pam's expressive face. 'After tomorrow, I shan't have to see him again, and I can forget the whole unfortunate episode.'

Pam pleaded, 'Aren't you going to tell me anything at all?'

'There's nothing to tell.'

'Spoilsport.' Pam's smile turned malicious. 'Then there's no point in my telling you anything about him. You wouldn't be interested.'

'Quite right,' Kim said, piqued by Pam's teasing when she herself had been deadly serious. 'Not the smallest bit interested.'

'Simone would be relieved to hear that.' Pam's smile was sly. 'She's really got her eye on him this time, so I'm told.'

'This time? Has she met him before, then?' Kim could have kicked herself for falling into the trap.

'Yes. Some years ago, though I doubt if *he'd* remember. She was just a spotty schoolgirl, so Georges tells me, when Lawrence came to spend a holiday with Georges. They met at the art college in Paris, where they both spent a year. They became close friends.'

'Georges is an artist too?' Kim was surprised. 'I thought he was a winemaker.'

'So he is; art was just another string to his bow.' Pam smiled smugly. 'But from now on, when he's not concentrating on me, he'll be concentrating on his wine.'

'And Lawrence Cory went on from art to architecture,' Kim said tightly. 'Let's hope it's better than his art.'

'Since you're not interested, it doesn't matter.' Pam's mind was still on the old track. 'But if you were, you'd have to fight hard to beat Simone.'

Kim stared at her friend in almost comical disbelief. 'Could you really imagine me in a battle with Simone over Lawrence Cory?' she asked derisively. 'Don't be ridiculous.'

Pam frowned, her brown eyes sweeping consideringly over Kim.

'Perhaps not,' she said at last. 'You're one sexy lady, Kim. But what Simone has in her favour is. . .determination.'

From where she sat, alongside Charles, in the flower-decked church, Kimberley could see Georges, his head turning anxiously every few moments towards the doorway through which he hoped Pamela would shortly arrive.

The bride was a few minutes late, but her appearance would be well worth the groom's wait, Kim knew. When she'd left Pam at the cottage half an hour before, she had looked unbelievably beautiful and surprisingly serene. Used to Pam's volatile reaction to most of life's events, Kim could only marvel at the change her love for Georges had wrought.

Her eyes misted a little as she realised that in an hour or so her lifelong friend would emerge from this old stone church to a new life as Mrs Georges Baron. . .a life which would irrevocably close the door on the past and on their long, close friendship.

They would keep in touch, of course, but things could never be the same again. It was a sobering thought, which did nothing to lift Kim's spirits.

Since that humiliating episode in the field she'd seen nothing of Lawrence Cory, until he'd walked into the church alongside Georges.

She hadn't been able to prevent her heart from missing a beat as he'd passed close by, looking impeccably handsome in his tail-coat, which fitted his lithe body to perfection.

Had he known she was there? Difficult to say, since he'd spared her not even a glance.

Simone, who was sitting further down in the church, had reached out and touched his hand as he'd passed and had been rewarded with a broad smile and a teasing wink.

One to Simone, Kim thought wryly, wondering if the French girl also thought there was some kind of contest between them. She would be in for a very pleasant surprise indeed when she discovered she had no competition.

Charles's hand touched gently against her arm, claiming her attention, and making her feel guilty. He'd arrived the night before. Georges had picked him up from the airport and taken him directly to Estelle's house to stay the night, and Kim had seen him for only a few moments outside the church, having left Pam behind with Georges's father, who, in the absence of her own father, was giving the bride away.

Music struck up, announcing the arrival of the bride, and everyone stood up. An air of excitement buzzed around the church and all eyes turned to the bride, who stood radiantly poised to walk down the aisle to join her dazzled groom.

The reception took place in the large marquee

erected in the grounds and the weather couldn't have been more glorious.

Kim, with Charles beside her, circulated among the guests, greeting the women she could recognise from the recent gathering.

She saw Lawrence Cory in the crowd; he was easy to spot since, for the most part, he stood head and shoulders above the shorter Frenchmen. She took pains to avoid coming face to face with him and hid herself in the crowd when he got up on the dais with Pam and Georges and his parents for the speeches.

His speech was light and wittily amusing, Kim admitted grudgingly, and she clapped with the rest.

He seemed to be avoiding contact with her as much as she with him, but, as he smilingly acknowledged the applause, his eyes swept around the room, coming to rest on her face. His mouth curled up at the corner and, to her consternation, he spoke to her directly in English.

'I see you still have your eyes open.'

Heads turned, eyes stared at her and laughter rippled around the room.

She felt her colour rise, and her heart hammered angrily against her ribs. How dared he single her out in that mocking way in front of all these people?

He was stepping down from the dais and seemed to be heading her way. If he came to her, she would probably lose her temper and let fly at him. She grasped Charles's arm hurriedly. 'Let's go outside for some fresh air.'

His face brightened. 'I could certainly do wth some. Was that fellow speaking to you?' he asked, as she led him to the exit.

'Why should he be?' she answered chillingly.

'I don't know,' he said doubtfully, eyeing her grim face with obvious trepidation.

It was a relief to be outside in the open, and she took deep steadying breaths as they slipped away into the deeper recesses of the garden.

'Lovely wedding,' Charles said, in an obvious attempt to break the ice, and Kim's heart softened.

Poor Charles. He hadn't a clue why his simple remark had led to her stony silence.

'It was beautiful,' she agreed, squeezing his arm contritely.

He smiled, his face gleaming faintly with perspiration. 'But it's much too hot for this damned monkey suit.'

Kim laughed. Charles, who was already beginning to spread a bit around the middle, looked as though he'd been stuffed into his formal grey suit.

'Take your jacket off,' she said. 'No one's going to notice here.'

They'd found an empty bench at last and Kim sank down gratefully, kicking off her black high-heeled shoes, which had begun to pinch.

'Why these shoes have to come to a point when my feet don't I'll never know.'

'Something to do with fashion, I expect,' Charles said seriously.

Kim laughed and kissed his cheek. He had a habit of taking practically everything literally, which could sometimes be endearing. 'I expect you're right.'

'Look,' he said suddenly, grasping her hand in his. 'I'm glad we've got this opportunity for a little private chat. I've got something I want to say to you.'

Kim frowned. He'd been unnaturally edgy ever since they'd got together earlier in the day. She'd known there was something on his mind and had taken a guess at what it might be. He'd been leading up to a proposal even before she'd left home, but she'd headed him off.

Kim bit her lip. The moment to pop the question had obviously arrived. The trouble was, she was far from ready to give him an answer. And somehow she didn't even want to hear the question from his lips.

'If you're going to propose, Charles,' she cut in quickly, 'I don't think now is the right time.'

Charles frowned. He said, with surprising insistence. 'Now seems the perfect time to me. I've been wanting to ask you for a long time, but. . .you know how it is. . .busy and all that. And then this wedding seemed to set the stage, as it were. What could be better guaranteed to put a woman in the mood for a proposal than her friend's wedding?' He kissed her hand with a little flourish. 'Marry me, Kim.'

Damn him! He'd said it! Kim was surprised to find she was more angry than flattered.

'No!' It came out more vehemently than she had intended. 'I'm not ready to think about marriage yet, Charles. I'm sorry.' She tried to soften the blow. 'But there's no rush, is there?'

'Isn't there?' His face was flushed, from more than the heat, his tone almost belligerent, Kim noted with disquiet. She had never seen Charles this way before. But then she'd never seen him display any other kind of strong emotion before either. His lack of temperament was one of the things she'd found so restful about him.

'Maybe not from your point of view. But from mine. . . I think it's more than time I told you how I feel about you. . .'

His arm went suddenly around Kim's shoulder and his fingers, hooking beneath her chin, turned her face to his. Before she could guess his intention, his mouth came down on hers, hot and demanding. He had kissed her before, but never like this, and, to her horror, she found it was unbearable.

Her lips shrank from his and a terrible sensation of icy revulsion filled the whole of her body. It was a feeling she'd experienced before and it was like reliving an old nightmare.

She pressed her hands against his chest, trying to push him away, but it only had the effect of increasing his ardour. His hold tightened, his lips began to move, his tongue probing into her mouth.

She gave a choked cry of protest, and he groaned.

'Kim,' he lifted his mouth to murmur raggedly against her ear. 'I didn't realise how much I wanted you. Until these last few days. . . I——'

'Let go of me, Charles. Please.' It was almost a sob. 'If you don't. . . I'll scream.'

'What?'

A light laugh sounded, searing across Kim's taut nerves.

Her head slewed in the direction of the sound and she saw two people strolling down the path. She gasped with horror as she recognised Simone, hanging on the arm of Lawrence Cory.

'Let go of me,' she whispered fiercely.

Charles moved back a little, bringing his flushed face into focus. His eyes seemed glazed as, slowly, he released her.

Simone came to a halt almost level with the bench on which they were sitting. 'Ah!' she exclaimed. 'It is little Pamela's friend. . .with yet another beau.' She looked with cynical amusement into Kim's stricken face.

'How fortunate you are, *chérie*, to have so many admirers.'

Kim's eyes shot to Lawrence Cory's cool face, expressionless but for the smallest lift of one eyebrow. Her own face burned with humiliation and, to her horror, she felt the brimming of unwilling tears.

'Excuse me.' Scooping up her shoes, she stood up hastily and, without even a glance at Charles, she hurried away up the path.

Though where she was headed was a mystery.

She could hardly rush into the house, tear-stained and looking for a haven.

Pam had gone up to one of the bedrooms some time ago to change into her going-away outfit. Even if she was there, Kim could hardly turn up in her present state.

Damn Charles!

She skirted the house, making for a set of outbuildings to the left of the premises, where she might find a little peace and quiet to restore her frayed nerves and cool her rising temper.

Damn Charles! She cursed him.

Damn that bitch Simone! And, most of all, damn Lawrence Cory!

He seemed to have a positive talent for turning up when and where she least expected him.

The outbuildings had been knocked together to form one large garage, housing at the moment two Land Rovers and the sleek sporty car she had driven in with Georges and Pam.

In one corner was a desk and two rather grimy-looking chairs.

Kim spread the scarf she'd been wearing around her shoulders on the seat of one of them and sat down.

A deep, shaky breath sighed through her trembling lips. What on earth was happening to her?

Charles, who had been her friend and almost-lover

for so long, had, in the space of a kiss, become a stranger. The sensation of his mouth against hers returned vividly, sending fresh waves of cold shuddering revulsion through her.

She closed her eyes.

The old nightmare was still with her. Philip holding her. . .kissing her. . .his hands tearing aside her clothes. . .grasping her breasts. . .

Oh, God! She groaned. Why did she keep putting herself through this? It was time the stupidity stopped.

Putting her elbows on to the table, she lowered her head into her hands. 'Ice-woman'.

Charles had resurrected her, she thought with a shudder, but somehow the spectre was no longer as real.

Hands touched her shoulders, making her start violently.

'Don't be frightened. It's only me.'

Kim looked up and groaned. 'Go away,' she said through clenched teeth. 'Why can't you leave me in peace?'

He'd turned her world upside-down and would give her no opportunity to right it again.

'Perhaps because you need a little help to find it.' Lawrence Cory drew her to her feet and pulled her gently towards him. 'Come here,' he commanded softly.

For some strange reason, she couldn't resist him.

Enclosing her in his arms, he pressed her head against his chest, his hands softly caressing her hair.

This felt so different, she realised with a kind of shock. . .his arms no prison, but a haven of warmth and comfort, his steady heartbeat a promise of security. . .

Why, when only moments before one man's kiss had

turned her to ice, should this man's tender hold set her body aflame? And yet, in some strange way, the sensation was equally unbearable.

It was idiotic that she could delude herself there was safety in the arms of a man like him.

'I'm fine now,' she said firmly.

Pulling herself out of his arms was like tearing herself in two, she thought in amazement, but it was something she had to do if he wasn't to guess at the power he seemed inexplicably to have acquired over her.

'Good.' He released her and looked down into her face. 'Want to talk about it?'

Kim flinched from him, her eyes becoming guarded. 'There's nothing to talk about.'

He gave an exasperated sigh and, with a gentle hand, swept the hair back from her face. 'You look a mess.'

'Thanks.'

The mock insult restored her balance, as it was probably intended to do, she realised with unwilling gratitude.

Tearing her gaze from his, she fished in the pocket of her light suit for her handkerchief and dabbed at her cheeks, embarrassed by the evidence of smudged mascara. He hadn't really been joking. 'I'd better go inside and tidy myself up.'

He nodded. 'Want me to come with you? I'll have a drink waiting for you when you come down from the bathroom.'

Kim shook her head. 'No, thanks.' She couldn't meet his gaze. 'I expect Charles will be wondering where I've got to.'

It was a deliberate effort to re-erect the barriers between them, and he knew it.

His mouth curled wryly. 'Yes. Wondering about that, among other things,' he said.

CHAPTER FIVE

THE house seemed to ring with emptiness. . .the result of too much activity over the past two days, Kim decided. The aftermath of a big occasion was always a bit of an anticlimax, but things would soon return to normal.

Charles had left after the reception, by an evening flight. He'd been uncharacteristically subdued and Kim had felt guilty. He'd tried to talk to her, but she had silenced him with the plea that she needed time to think.

'I suppose I could arrange to stay an extra day,' he said doubtfully. 'It would mean rearranging some pretty important meetings, but I'd do it if you wanted me to.'

'I know. But it wouldn't help. I promise I'll think about things while I'm here, and when I get home we'll talk.'

He hadn't been able to hide his relief that she'd turned down his gesture, she remembered a little cynically. She wandered into the living-room—her favourite room in the whole cottage—and her eyes swept around, dwelling on the leaded bay windows, soft chintz-covered sofas and warm red-patterned carpet with a sense of appreciation. It was a lovely cottage, with an atmosphere of tranquillity that made her feel people had been happy there.

Crossing the wide room, she opened the windows and then turned on the radio. Music floated on to the fresh, summer-scented air, which wafted against the curtains and into the room.

A girl was singing in English; it was an old love-song.

Kim hurried to switch it off. The last thing she wanted on her mind at this moment was love. And the words seemed to fit too exactly to her recent experience with Lawrence Cory. Not that it had been a fling exactly—which was what the song was about—but it might have been if he'd had his way. Kim had sensed the danger. His charisma had been more powerful than she had wanted to admit and, despite her defences, he'd begun to get under her skin.

She hadn't spoken to him again after the incident in the garage, but, before he'd let her go alone up to the house, he had taken her in his arms and kissed her gently, undemandingly, filling her with a yearning sensation all the more painful because it brought no promise of fulfilment.

Pamela's fantasy of romance and marriage between them was just that. . .a fantasy. The magic he seemed able to weave about her was as insubstantial as gossamer. She'd be crazy to think it was anything else.

Her lips burned suddenly with the memory of his mouth against hers and she touched her fingers wonderingly against the delicate skin. Had he gone on holding her, deepened his kiss, would she have managed to resist him?

What was it the stars had foretold? 'A stranger's act of kindness could be the beginning of a beautiful friendship'. Something like that.

So much for forecasts, she thought wryly.

The stranger had done his good deed and disappeared, without even saying goodbye, for which blessing she would be eternally grateful.

But, annoyingly, the holiday she'd looked forward to seemed suddenly pointless.

She toyed with the idea of leaving the cottage, of going back to work. That, more than anything, could be guaranteed to return her to normal, but Charles would be waiting for her and she was in no mood to deal with him in his present frame of mind.

She felt uncharacteristically drained . . .

Perhaps she would feel better after a night's sleep.

Much to her surprise, Kim slept deeply and late. The sun was shining warmly on her pillow when she finally awoke. For a moment, she panicked, feeling there was some urgency about the day, but as she became aware of her surroundings she relaxed. There was no urgency about anything. The day was her own.

It was a further surprise to find that the blues of the previous day had disappeared, which made her feel optimistic.

She stretched luxuriously, taking her time about getting out of bed. Even indoors it was already warm, and the sound of birds singing drew her to the window. The sun was high in a brilliantly clear sky. By midday it would be scorching, and already she was longing for a swim. Later, she might take a stroll down to the beach.

Her bedroom, smaller and cosier than the one Pam had used, faced the rear garden. Kim sat in the window-seat, gazing across the expanse of lawn to the small wood at the bottom. Beyond that screen of trees, Pam had told her, was a stream and the relic of the old mill building.

There hadn't been time for Pam to show her around, but later, she thought, with a little spurt of excitement, she would go down there and explore.

A flash of something white caught her eye in the vicinity of the old wooden summer-house, which was tucked away at the bottom of the garden. She sat upright and peered intently through the window, but could see nothing obvious. Bushes to the right of the little wooden building were moving and it was possible that what she'd seen was the sun's reflection on the leaves. But the explanation left her uneasy. What if there was an intruder in the garden? Highly unlikely, she chided herself derisively. But—perhaps—not impossible. . .

Kim snorted irritably. She wasn't the nervous type who imagined that every unaccountable sound or movement spelled danger. She stood up determinedly. The best way to put her mind at rest was to go down there to investigate.

Slipping quickly into shorts and a T-shirt, she went down the narrow stairs and out into the garden. Barefoot, because she'd forgotten her sandals, she ran lightly across the lawn, slowing as she reached the summer-house.

She looked about, feeling furtive and foolish. What was she expecting to see?

Slowly she began to move nearer, to be stopped in her tracks by a sound, startling her pulse into frantic activity. Her gaze followed the sound and she saw the flash of white again. A curtain flapping at the open window of the summer-house.

Kim let out the breath she hadn't known she'd been holding and felt relief flooding through her. She gave a shaky laugh. Pamela must have opened the windows to air the place out and her *intruder* was a curtain.

Fear had wound her up. . .relief invigorated her. She walked on past the summer-house towards the mill, her bare feet sinking deliciously into the cool dewy grass. She had to pick her way more carefully through the bracken of the narrow wood, but soon she was out on to the gentle slope which led down to the stream. Here, the hot sun had already warmed the ground. It scorched down on her head, penetrating her clothes to heat her body, and it was a relief to reach the shade of the willow trees which grew along the banks.

The water was cold against her feet as she stepped from the bank on to a flat, rocky shelf. She gasped with shock and then laughed. She'd been longing for a swim and, since the stream was deep enough, there was no time like the present. Impulsively, she peeled off her T-shirt and shorts and threw them on to the bank, then, lowering herself into the water, she began to swim with slow, lazy strokes, revelling in the silky movement of the water against her skin.

Further down, the banks rose and the bed dropped sharply into a basin formed by two rocky outcrops.

This was as far as she'd go, she decided, and turned to rest on her back, floating with her eyes closed against the light of the sun.

A splash sounded nearby, as though a stone had fallen into the water, and she felt the movement of ripples against her body. Startled, she turned over and squinted her eyes against the bright reflection. A dark head bobbed on the surface some forty yards away and brown arms cleared the water in a powerful over-arm stroke that told her the swimmer was a man.

Kim's first reaction was a stab of annoyance. For all she knew, this part of the stream might belong with his property, but his presence resurrected her uneasy fears. Had it been the summer-house curtain she'd seen from her bedroom window, or had this intruder also been in the garden and followed her?

For a moment, anger overcame her fear, and she began to swim towards him bent on challenging him. She stopped mid-stroke as she remembered she was stark naked.

Ducking beneath the water, she moved closer to the high bank. The water was thicker here and she had to screw up her eyes, concentrating on peering through the murk. A jagged rock loomed with sudden menace before her, startling her into taking in water. She surfaced hurriedly, spluttering and choking, to stare into concerned amber eyes.

'Are you all right?' There was a deep frown between Lawrence Cory's dark brows.

Kim's eyes bulged with indignation and the choking effort to cough the vile water from her lungs.

'Take it easy,' he advised kindly. 'Here, let me tow you in.'

He turned her adroitly and hooked an arm beneath hers, bringing the back of her head against his shoulder, lifting her face clear of the water as he swam with powerful movements of his legs and free arm.

Kim let him take her. There wasn't much else she could do with spasms of coughing still racking her body.

He held on to her until he'd hauled her on to a flat rock, and then released her.

'That could have been nasty,' he said. 'I thought you were making a mistake. . .swimming that close to the rocks.' He swept his wet hair back from his face. 'Good job I was on the spot.'

Kim coughed the last of the water from her lungs and faced him with streaming eyes.

'I got into problems *because* you were on the spot,' she gritted furiously. 'What on earth are you *doing* here?'

'Explanations later,' he said firmly. 'But for now I think we could both do with a nice hot cup of tea.'

He stood up and it was then Kim realised he was as naked as herself, his muscular body gleaming wet and powerful, towering over her as she sat on her ledge.

She stared up at him, speechless with embarrassment, feeling the rush of blood to her face.

He looked down at her and laughed. 'Adam and Eve,' he teased. 'Only without the fig leaves.'

He gave her no time to answer—not that she could have done. . .Hauling her to her feet, he lifted her up into his arms.

Kim buried her crimson face in the hollow of his shoulder as he walked with her towards the house. If she even tried to visualise the picture they must present, she knew she would simply melt away with the terrible humiliation.

Her shivering had subsided, but her throat was raw and aching. She would probably catch some dreadful virus from swallowing that revolting water, she thought dismally, as she watched Lawrence Cory throw another log on to the fire and push it down among the others with the poker.

He'd set light to the logs in the grate, despite the warmth of the day, and Kim was ensconced on the sofa, wrapped in a blanket, a cup of hot sweet tea clasped in her hands.

She'd argued that she didn't take sugar, but he'd insisted,

'Drink it. Sugar's good for shock.'

She felt the old resentment at his high-handedness, but sipped her tea silently for a while, feeling the warmth reach down inside, reviving her spirits.

'Now,' she said firmly, as she regained some of her

old forcefulness, 'I'd like an answer to my question. What are you doing here at the cottage?'

He was sitting on the floor, his back leaning against the sofa, looking pensively into the fire.

She could have reached out and touched him, but tucked her free hand into the blanket, out of harm's way. When both hands were free she might wring his neck.

'I don't think you're going to like the answer,' he said at last.

Kim felt a trickle of apprehension along her spine and, for some reason, Pamela's laughing face rose before her eyes.

'Then you'd better tell me quickly and get it over with.'

Oddly, it seemed impossible to take her eyes off him. He'd been naked when he'd brought her into the house, but somewhere he'd found a pair of shorts which showed his brown muscular thighs and a cotton sweatshirt which seemed moulded to his body.

'Like you, I'm here on holiday for a couple more weeks,' he said slowly. 'And Pam said I can share the cottage with you.'

'Pam said what?' Kim's voice rose to a shriek.

He grinned. 'I told you you wouldn't like it.'

'Well, you're right,' she gritted. 'There is no way we could live together in this house without. . .'

She tailed off, caught by the mocking gleam in his cool eyes.

'Without murdering one another?' he suggested.

'Precisely,' Kim agreed tightly, although it wasn't exactly what she had been thinking. She'd been thinking. . . 'And there is no way I will agree to sharing this cottage with you.'

He nodded. 'I thought that would be your reaction.

So I've come up with a compromise, which I think will suit us both. I've taken over the little summer-house.'

'Have you thought that it might be a compromise that doesn't suit me? I don't want you here. Is that plain enough?'

He sighed. 'I wish I knew why I'm such a leper.'

'And I wish I knew what you're doing here,' Kim hit back in rising fury. 'And how you manage to keep turning up when and where I least expect you.'

'Lucky coincidence,' he suggested, straight-faced but with a mocking glimmer in his eyes.

'Coincidence carefully organised between yourself and Pamela,' she accused him. 'And don't bother to deny it because she's admitted it to me already.'

'That's interesting. Am I allowed to know what she admitted?'

'Don't play the innocent,' she shot at him.

He raised one brow provocatively. 'Isn't that what I'm supposed to be. . .innocent—until proven guilty?'

'She told you I'd be coming over on the same ferry and arranged with you to pick me up.' Kim's breath shortened with heightened indignation. 'She probably gave you the impression that I was just panting to be swept off my feet by the first good-looking man who was kind enough to notice me.'

His eyes widened in a good imitation of astonishment. 'For a beautiful woman, you seem to have precious little self-esteem, Kimberley.' He laughed shortly. 'From my experience, I'd say you were anything but a push-over.'

Kim bit her lip, wishing she could believe he was genuine.

'And, being you're a close friend,' he went on, 'I'm sure Pamela would know that.'

'Pamela knows only what she wants to know,' Kim

said shortly. 'She's got some astrological bee in her bonnet about me being a too-critical Virgo, destined to become a cold and lonely virgin, unless I learn to compromise. She's been throwing one man after another at my head ever since——'

She stopped short, stunned by the realisation that she had been about to give away to him the secret of her past.

'Since your last unhappy love-affair?' he finished for her.

Kim gasped and gave a hasty swallow. 'Pamela told you about Philip Crossley,' she said thickly. 'She swore to me that she hadn't.'

'She didn't need to.' He smiled ironically. 'Every bitter woman has at least one unhappy love-affair in her past.'

'I'm not bitter,' Kim denied, angered by the shake in her voice. 'I just intend to make sure that, when I do marry, it will be to the *right* man.'

He nodded gravely. 'And is your friend Charles the *right* man?'

Hot colour surged into Kim's cheeks. 'Probably,' she said tightly. 'Not that it's any of your business.'

'True.' He nodded. 'Except that I wouldn't want you to compromise and chalk up another mistake.'

Kim started as though he had activated every raw nerve in her body. Her eyes were stinging with unshed tears. 'And there ends my latest session on the couch, Dr Cory,' she said with heavy sarcasm. 'I don't think I'll be troubling you for another.'

She stood up abruptly, hitching the blanket more securely about her.

His gaze swept over her, seeming to penetrate the thick folds of blanket that swathed her naked body, reminding her of what he had seen before he'd wrapped her up. There was no mistaking the warmth in his amber eyes, the sensuousness in the curving smile, and Kim's heart leapt into lurching response to their unspoken challenge.

'If you don't mind, I'd like to take a shower.'

'I don't mind,' he said, seemingly unperturbed. 'As long as there's some hot water left for me.'

'You?' she said breathlessly. 'You don't still think I'm going to let you. . .'

His brows drew together in a swift frown.

'Look here, Miss cool, critical Virgo,' he said, his voice unexpectedly cold, 'I don't need your permission.'

He gripped her arm, his fingers biting hard into the soft flesh. 'For the sake of your acute sensibilities, I've given up a legitimate and comfortable bed for a draughty summer-house, and that's as far as I'm prepared to give. The other facilities we share fifty-fifty.'

CHAPTER SIX

KIM had been a long time in the shower and had taken even longer to dry herself, postponing the moment when she would have to go downstairs to face Lawrence Cory again.

For some reason, she felt ridiculously vulnerable. Used as she was now to running her own business, having things done her way, it had been an uncomfortable shock to realise that, in this situation, she and Lawrence Cory were equals and he was under no obligation to act in accordance with any rules that she might devise.

Reluctant as she was to go downstairs, she was drawn at last by the delicious smells which wafted up, stimulating her appetite.

He was in the kitchen, looking very much at home as he busied himself at the stove.

Her first feelings were those of outrage.

'When you suggested sharing fifty-fifty,' she said irritably, 'I hardly expected to find you've got the run of the house.'

'Hardly the run of the house to be using the kitchen,' he responded with maddening calm. 'I can't make myself totally invisible, and I do have to eat.'

'Where did you find the food?' she asked sourly. 'The last time I looked, the cupboard was almost empty.'

'It isn't now,' he said. 'I brought a box of groceries along earlier.'

Kim frowned. He really was making himself at home.

'You didn't have to do that. I intended doing some shopping later today.'

'I didn't bring them for you.' He shot her a wry glance over his shoulder. 'But if you want to share some with me now, you can pay me back later.'

He saw her startled look and laughed. 'Not in kind, of course. I meant by cooking me a meal from the groceries you intend to buy.'

Kim sniffed the air. Something was smelling delicious. 'What's cooking?' she asked with unwilling interest.

'Spanish omelette, with jacket potatoes and a salad.'

He'd already set two places at the scrubbed wooden table, Kim noted, but she made no comment.

'Sounds great,' she admitted, feeling suddenly ravenous. 'But what's that enticing aroma?'

'Garlic bread.'

He bent down to open the oven door and brought forth a well-browned loaf. 'How's that?' He grinned and shot her a look of self-satisfaction. 'Not bad, eh?'

'Incredible,' she admitted grudgingly. 'Did you really bake it yourself?'

'But of course.' He shrugged with a very French gesture. 'For fifteen minutes in the oven. . .as per instructions from René, our wonderful village baker.'

'A part-baked loaf!' Kim couldn't help but laugh. 'Well, at least you're honest. I might have been tempted to tell a little white lie and claim all the credit for myself.' She sat down at the table. 'The heater's still on for the shower if you want one.' The concessions had begun, she thought wryly. But one had to start somewhere.

He turned a large omelette out on to a heated plate and cut it into two. 'Let's eat first. I'm starving.'

He put one half of the omelette on to another plate

and handed it to her. He brought the food to the table, putting the bread on the board and tipping potatoes into a basket.

'Help yourself.'

Kim saw the flexion of his thigh muscles as he flung his leg across the bench and sat down opposite her.

He busied himself forking a large potato from the basket on to his plate, all his concentration seemingly focused on splitting it and piling butter into the aperture.

Kim cut a piece of her omelette and popped it into her mouth. It was absolutely delicious, light and fluffy and seasoned to perfection. She applied herself to another mouthful and chewed slowly and appreciatively.

He was eating with absorbed enjoyment and she studied him across the table.

'You're obviously a man of many talents,' she said. 'Quite honestly, I'm not sure what to make of you.'

He looked up. 'Don't you? What's the problem?'

'No *problem*,' she answered with a little frown. 'It's just that you seem able to adapt to any background. Perfectly at home wherever you find yourself. It's disconcerting.'

He grinned. 'But all part of my charm.'

'I wouldn't put it quite like that.' Kim grimaced. 'You're incredibly conceited.'

He cut a piece of potato and carried it to his mouth, chewing pensively for a while before he spoke. 'I can see how things might appear that way,' he said judiciously. 'But in reality, I'm well aware of my limitations.'

'I'm relieved to hear it.'

'You, on the other hand, seem unconscious even of your most basic potential. If you should require help to explore new avenues of experience, remember. . . I'm available.'

Kim choked on the food she'd just put into her mouth and glared at him indignantly. 'Let's get one thing straight!' she exploded, when she could speak. 'My *potential* is my own—not included in the shared facilities. I do not intend to become an open book into which you feel fully entitled to delve as the mood takes you.'

'OK.' He shook his head. 'But you don't have to be a closed book either.'

Kim laughed derisively. 'That's good. . .coming from you. You led me to believe you were an artist, but that's only a sideline, isn't it? In reality you're the architect who's going to renovate Pam and Georges's house. The one Pam has designs on for my life partner. You obviously didn't feel it necessary to tell me that.'

Calmly, he studied her irate face.

'I wasn't aware of Pam's designs,' he said coolly. 'And, as for the way I earn my living, you told me you weren't interested.' He shrugged. 'Why waste information on someone who doesn't want it?'

Kim, ignoring the latter gibe, challenged him.

'If you weren't aware of what Pamela was planning, why were you so determined to get together with me on the journey down?'

'Was I?' he asked with that maddening lift of his dark brows. 'No more determined than I would have been with any other beautiful and intriguing woman.'

Her smile was cynical. 'Is that what I am? Beautiful and intriguing?'

He shook his head and put down his knife and fork to give her his undivided attention. 'There you go again! Retreating behind that high wall. Why? Don't you like being told you're beautiful?'

'Perhaps,' she said stubbornly. 'By the right man.'

He sighed irritably. 'Well, let's hope you find Mr Right. Given your present attitude, he wouldn't get within a mile of you. And if he had any sense he'd give up and go away before he froze to death.'

He picked up his knife and fork and absorbed himself once again in his meal, his expression one of total indifference.

'Oh!' Kim growled frustratedly. 'You're impossible.'

She pushed her plate away and scraped back her chair, ready to rise, but he reached across the table and grasped her wrist.

'Stay put and eat your food,' he commanded. 'You can't expect to win every little skirmish. And you don't have to sulk every time you lose.' His eyes met her wide angry gaze steadily.

'I'm not sulking!' she blazed. 'But you're right about one thing: I don't have to *do* anything. You're determined to stay here, but I don't have to put up with you.'

He nodded slowly. 'You don't. But why not give it a try? You might find it has its compensations.'

She gave a short cynical laugh. 'Am I allowed to guess what those might be?'

With a gesture that startled her, he stood up suddenly, reaching across the table to grasp her shoulders and pull her to her feet.

'Why guess?' he said, his voice dangerously soft. 'When I can just as easily demonstrate?'

In one movement, he was around the table and had pulled her into his arms, holding her so tightly that she couldn't pull away. He bent his head and crushed his mouth against hers.

There was no pleasure in his kiss, only a painful,

unwilling excitement, which burned through her body and inflamed her mind to fury.

Jerking backwards, she tore her mouth from his. 'You're hurting me,' she gasped.

He glared at her, his face startlingly grim and intent. 'Maybe that's the only way to get through to you.'

He grabbed her back into his arms, kissing her fiercely.

Trapped by his steely strength, Kim could only fume.

How dared he do this? How dared he force her to confront the fact that, where he was concerned, there was only heat? In his arms, even with his lips brutally punishing hers, 'ice-woman' could only melt. As the kiss went on, rigid fury threatened to give way to reluctant wonder.

His hand was inside the thin material of her T-shirt, moving urgently against the silky-smooth skin of her back. She heard his breathing quicken and her own stifled gasp as his fingers slipped the catch of her bra and slid around to her breast.

She shivered as they made contact with her aroused flesh and he groaned, relaxing the taut grasp of his arm about her waist. The movement of his hand became softly urgent, his mouth tender, searching, moving from her lips to the column of her throat.

Locked in his arms, on the edge of surrender, she knew she wanted to go on. . .exploring the exquisite sensations aroused by the circling motion against her breast, allowing the strange tide of feeling to go on rising from deep within her. . . But she didn't dare.

Gathering the remnants of her strength, she flinched from him, her hand coming up to cover his. . .to stop the caress which was driving her mad.

'No. Stop!' Her voice was broken with emotion, pitched high and unfamiliar.

He slackened his hold on her, standing back a little to see into her face. His own was flushed, his eyes bright with undisguised passion, his chest rising and falling unevenly.

'What. . .happened. . .?' He seemed almost dazed. 'I thought——'

'I know what you thought. . .' she cut in harshly, lowering her head. 'And I'm sorry to disappoint you.'

She heard the anger in his brief laugh.

'I'm not disappointed.' His hands were on her shoulders. 'I didn't want anything you didn't.' He shook her fiercely, making her look up at him. 'Damn it, woman, admit it!'

Kim felt the trembling of her lip and bit it. 'Let go of me, please,' she pleaded. 'I can't think.'

Releasing her shoulders, he cupped her face in his hands. 'Don't *think*, Kim. *Feel!*' He brushed her lips lingeringly with his. 'How did that make you *feel*?'

As if she were drowning, she thought in sudden panic.

She swallowed back the lump which had risen in her throat and said helplessly, 'I don't know. I can't reason when you look at me like that.'

He snorted impatiently. 'Then I'll go on looking at you like that until I get an answer to my question.'

Suddenly Kim was angry. 'I have no answer. And I'm sick of your bullying. . .having to fight you every step of the way just to get a little peace.'

He let her go suddenly and stood back with a sigh. 'OK. I agree it's a battle.' He sat down again at the table. 'So why don't we call a truce? I promise I'll keep out of your way as much as possible. If that's what you want.'

'That's what I want,' Kim affirmed shakily.

She couldn't stay. Her whole being was in danger of collapse.

She left him shaking his head and staring after her, his broad shoulders drooping defeatedly.

She'd won, but somehow it was a hollow victory and in some way she seemed to be the loser.

Lawrence Cory was nowhere in sight as Kim came out into the garden with a blanket, cushion and a book, prepared to do a little serious sunbathing.

True to his word, he'd kept out of her way for the last three days. On the odd occasion that they had coincided, his greeting had been pleasant but brief.

He seemed to be taking care not to use the kitchen when she did and she was left to assume that he took breakfast very early before she had risen and bathed either late at night or before breakfast. She had, on occasion, heard the water running and had once been tempted to go to the bathroom door and shout to him to stop being so childish. Avoiding her in this obvious way made her all the more annoyingly aware of his presence.

But she'd fought the urge and was relieved that she had. There was no way she was going to let him know that this shunning left her feeling lonely and rejected. The whole situation was ridiculous.

She read a little and then withdrew into the shade to rest.

The garden was empty and very still as though even the birds had taken refuge from the hot sun, and so sharp had her senses become where Lawrence Cory was concerned that she could tell he wasn't anywhere about. He'd gone out yet again, without a word.

Of course, he was under no obligation to inform her of his comings and goings, she acknowledged irritably, but she nevertheless felt peeved. If only he'd tell her when he was going out, she'd be able to relax and enjoy her solitude, without having to be on pins all the time, wondering if and when he was going to show up again.

She moved restlessly and sighed.

For some reason, she felt wound-up and full of nervous energy, and lying here quietly in the sun was no longer as appealing as it had been. She got up and wandered back to the house and into the kitchen.

She was hungry, but unable to decide on what to have for lunch. Fresh provisions were getting low and she'd been too lethargic to do even the necessary shopping. The village shops were attractive, but of the small local variety. There would obviously be more choice in one of the supermarkets of the small town, which was only about half an hour's drive away. Perhaps there she'd find something to tempt her appetite. Or she could even find a little restaurant and treat herself to a meal.

She began to feel more positive.

The prospect of getting away from the cottage for a few hours was suddenly energising. And while she was in town she could take the opportunity for a little sightseeing. Pam had mentioned a small cathedral that was worth a visit.

Walking around the little town, Kim felt a rise in spirits. Her shopping completed and stowed in the boot of her car, she set off to find the cathedral. She found it in a little side-turning off the high street, rising above the strangely medieval-looking little shops which clustered in its shadow. The shop fronts had obviously been renovated, but this had been done tastefully and in keeping with their history.

She wondered who the architect had been and thought of Lawrence Cory.

Then, as though the thought had conjured him up, she saw him. Through the window of one of the little shops, he could be seen deep in conversation with a short dark man. He was wearing a suit, and Kim was struck again by his confident good looks. She wondered what he was doing there and then remembered that Pamela had told her he was thinking of buying a business in this little town.

The shop fronts were deceptive. Inside, the building was very much modern-day. The ground-floor room was open plan and went back a long way. Kim could see a number of drawing-boards towards the rear of the rather grand reception area, each with its own little territory, marked by large stone pots of leafy green plants.

The whole thing was very impressive, and Kim wondered what decision Lawrence would make.

Not that it was of any interest to her, she thought, realising suddenly that she had been blatantly peering through the window. Mercifully, Lawrence was too absorbed to notice, but the receptionist was peering back at Kim and seemed about to draw someone's attention to her presence.

Hurriedly, she walked past and hastened down the road into the front entrance of the cathedral. The last thing she wanted now was for Lawrence Cory to think she had followed him and, to all appearances, had been blatantly spying on him.

The cathedral interior was cool and smelled of polish and incense. A light burned on the central altar and a service was in progress, attended by a small group of worshippers, mainly old men and women, devoutly fingering their rosaries.

Kim felt like an intruder, but knelt quietly in the deserted pews of a small side-altar, gaining time to allow any curiosity she might have aroused to die down. After a little while the peace of the place began to descend upon her and she knelt and closed her eyes.

Half an hour later, she came across an intriguing little restaurant in one of the many side-streets, and found herself a table for one in a discreet corner close to the quaintly mullioned windows.

She ordered a meal of veal in a rich cheese sauce, with fresh vegetables, and sat awaiting its arrival, gazing out on to the little street, feeling relaxed and comfortable for the first time in days.

But it wasn't to last. A couple turned the corner and crossed the cobbled street, heading straight for the front door of the restaurant, and Kim groaned. The man was Lawrence Cory and the woman was Simone.

Damn! Kim cursed furiously. How did he manage it? No matter where she chose to go, he could be guaranteed to make a beeline directly there. It was uncanny and annoying, and made her wonder whether she gave off some kind of radar which only he seemed capable of picking up.

Kim chewed at her lip in frustration, which turned to self-disgust when she felt her pulse-rate rise sharply as the door opened and Lawrence and Simone entered.

She looked around desperately for a means of escape. There was a door to the rear of the room which probably led out into the kitchen, but she could hardly go barging in there. Besides, she would have to cross an unnervingly wide expanse of very public space before she could reach that unsafe haven.

What on earth's the matter with you? she admonished herself irritably. You were here first and have every bit as much right to be here as he has. . .they have. . .

It infuriated her still more to realise that she needn't have worried anyway, since neither of them noticed her tucked away in her little corner. Lawrence had his hand in the crook of Simone's arm and was leading her towards a little corner of their own, discreetly screened by the inevitable greenery. Before they sat down and out of her sight, Kim saw the look of inviting admiration in Simone's cat-like eyes and the indulgent smile which curved Lawrence Cory's sensuous mouth as he looked back at her.

The girl obviously hadn't wasted much time in hunting down her quarry, Kim thought bitchily, remembering what Pamela had told her about Simone's determination to capture Lawrence's attention. She's certainly managed that easily enough, the mean little inner voice added sourly.

Was that what he had been hoping for from her? Kim wondered furiously. Unquestioning admiration. . .unresisting surrender. . .

A disturbing vision rose before her inner eye of Simone locked ecstatically in Lawrence Cory's arms, experiencing the same searing sensations which had speared through her own body as his lips devoured hers. . .

'Your veal, *mademoiselle*. May I serve?'

Kim started at the sound of the waiter's polite voice and flushed to the roots of her hair in embarrassment. What must she have looked like, staring across at a screen of plants, trying with X-ray vision to see what lay beyond?

'I'm sorry,' she said, forcing a smile. 'I was miles away.'

And as she sat before the carefully prepared meal,

with all trace of hunger having evaporated, she wished she were just that. Miles away from the conflicting and confusing emotions which were currently playing havoc with her nervous system.

But fate was obviously in a whimsical mood.

As she sat toying with the food on her plate, the restaurant door opened once more and the short dark man Kim had seen in conversation with Lawrence Cory entered, followed closely by the woman receptionist.

Kim's fork slipped from her suddenly nerveless fingers and, as it clattered against her plate, the woman's head slewed in her direction. Kim's blood froze as she saw recognition dawning in the bright blue eyes.

The woman nudged her companion and spoke to him. He shot a curious glance in Kim's direction, before shrugging his shoulders and urging her, with an impatient gesture, towards Lawrence's table.

Kim was maddened by the screen of foliage; it was impossible to see what was going on and trying to guess was an agony of frustration. But she didn't have to guess for long. Lawrence's head appeared above the plants as he stood up.

Her heart sank, but, with determination born of fatalism, she'd managed to pin a cool smile on her face just as he turned and caught her gaze.

His expression was unreadable, but, even from this distance, she thought she saw a gleam of mockery in his eyes.

She nodded a brief acknowledgement, hoping he would have the sensitivity to spare her feelings by leaving it at that. But, as she might have guessed, he came towards her.

'Why, Kimberley!' he said warmly. 'How nice. This is an unexpected surprise. Won't you join us?'

Somehow, Kim managed to keep her smile intact

and her gaze steady on his. 'That's kind of you, but I won't disturb you. I was just about to leave.'

'Nonsense,' he said firmly. 'We're having a little celebration. I'm sure you can spare us a few moments of your time.'

Kim's expression hardened. 'I really don't think I can.'

She cast a sideways glance towards his table and gasped as she was caught up in Simone's narrowed green stare. The girl was on her feet and staring across at them, and she was obviously livid.

Turning her attention back to Lawrence Cory, she said in a tight, furious whisper, 'Will you stop trying to humiliate me?'

'On the contrary.' He lowered his voice. 'I'm trying to save your face. Madame Daumier is under the impression that you're some kind of female peeping Tom. I think you should make the effort to disabuse her.' He hooked his hand firmly beneath her elbow. 'I'll get the waiter to move your stuff.'

'Don't bother.' Kim capitulated with a sigh. 'I couldn't eat another thing.'

'Madame and Monsieur Daumier,' Lawrence said, and Kim nodded politely.

Madame Daumier's lively face was full of curiosity as Lawrence made the introduction.

'This is Miss Kimberley Harris,' he said in his flawless French. 'We are currently sharing Mill Cottage.'

There was a stunned silence, as the woman's gaze went from Kim to Simone's furious face and back again.

Kim froze in consternation. What a way to effect an introduction. Her face flamed as *madame's* dark brows rose and her husband smiled a knowing little smile.

'I have the house and Mr Cory has the summer-house,' she explained, trying to keep the indignation from her voice, adding with a hint of malice, 'Actually, we're practically strangers.'

Simone's tinkling laugh sounded. 'A situation I'm sure you are doing your best to remedy, *chérie*!' She arched her brows disdainfully.

Kim opened her mouth to deliver a cutting retort, but shut it again as she met Lawrence Cory's wry glance and the faint warning shake of his head.

He would pay for this, she vowed grimly, glaring at him.

Impervious, he pulled out a chair for Kim. 'Won't you sit down?'

Kim sat, uncomfortably aware that Simone's gaze was pinned resentfully on her.

'Monsieur and Madame Daumier have just agreed to sell their business to me,' Lawrence said lightly. 'Hence the little celebration I just mentioned.'

Kim flushed. So the lady wasn't a receptionist after all, she was the dapper little Frenchman's wife. Somehow it made the 'peeping Tom' episode even more embarrassing. Goodness knew what the pair were silently making of this peculiar situation. They probably thought the English were mad.

But Lawrence Cory's news had almost taken her breath away, and she couldn't hide her surprise. 'You mean. . .you've already decided?'

'Yes.' He shot her a look of pleased satisfaction. 'The business seems just what I'm looking for and I've fallen in love with the area.'

The gleaming amber eyes seemed to be relaying to her a special message, but Kim shook the silly notion away.

She sighed a little sigh of relief. He was staying in France, which meant that when she left for home. . .!

'It. . .didn't take you long to. . .make up your mind.'

Why did she feel so nervous? she wondered irritably. Perhaps it had something to do with Simone's antagonism, which was hanging in the atmosphere, so thick you could cut it with a knife. Only Lawrence seemed oblivious.

'That's true,' he agreed cheerfully. 'But then, quick decisions are part of my nature. Once I've made up my mind about something, I don't see any sense in hanging about. Typical Gemini, so I believe.'

He was teasing her, Kim knew, reminding her of her ill-advised mention of astrology, which, if she remembered rightly, had predicted his success in business and a stormy time in love. Well, if Simone's tempestuous face was anything to go by, the prediction would be spot-on in that respect.

'I wouldn't know,' she said tightly. And, because that sounded a little surly, she added, 'Well! I wish you luck.'

He laughed, and summoned the waiter to bring another glass, filling it with champagne and handing it to her. 'Let's drink to that.'

The celebration wasn't exactly a success. The Daumier couple's spirits were obviously dampened by the undercurrents of hostility flowing from Simone to Kim.

Not that Kim could entirely blame the girl. She had come out for dinner with Lawrence, hoping to be alone with him, only to find they were surrounded by people who diverted his attention from herself.

As soon as she decently could, Kim decided, she would leave them all to it.

She did her best, calling on her business experience

of difficult situations to pull her through. She asked about the history of their little town. The Daumiers answered initially with enthusiastic pride, but Kim could see their enthusiasm waning in the face of Simone's wooden refusal to take part in any discussion about her home town.

Perhaps things would improve when she left, Kim thought irritably—there was little point in enduring any more of this rather fraught celebration.

'If you'll excuse me,' she said at last, 'I must go. I'm. . .expecting a telephone call at home.'

It wasn't really a lie. Charles had said he would telephone some time this week. Not that she was looking forward to his call, but it made a convenient excuse for the moment.

Simone's face brightened, but not for long.

'If you're going back to the cottage,' Lawrence said, 'I could use a lift.' He grinned at Kim. 'If you like, I could stand outside with my thumb up. Or I could always change your tyre.'

Why was he reminding her of the manner of their meeting? she speculated. Was it his way of saying he always got his own way in the end?

'That won't be necessary,' Kim said coolly, ignoring the intimate gleam in his amber eyes. 'But are you sure you wouldn't rather stay on with your friends and then take a taxi later?'

'There is no need for a taxi. I have my car and I will drive you, Lawrie,' Simone cut in a little sulkily.

Kim noted the familiar shortening of his name. When and where, she wondered, had they become so chummy?

'Surely we don't have to rush off?' Simone coaxed, her head tilted invitingly. 'This is a celebration. I would like to eat dessert and have a coffee.'

Lawrence patted the long fingers she was drumming on the table. 'Another time, Simone. But I too have to use the telephone. There are a number of calls I must make to tie up the purchase of the Daumier business.'

Monsieur Daumier lifted his shoulders and spread his hands. 'Oh! But I should be delighted to give you the use of my office telephone.'

'Many thanks.' Lawrence's smile was growing a little fixed. 'But I don't have the necessary paperwork to hand. It will be more convenient at the cottage.'

Kim noted the signs of temper; the tight frown and the white lines of tension about his mouth. He was hating having to argue his decision.

Monsieur Daumier, also reading Lawrence's expression correctly, shrugged and spread his hands. 'In that case, we mustn't keep you.'

Lawrence relaxed visibly. He smiled coaxingly and leaned across to kiss Simone's pouting mouth.

'I'll make it up to you, *mon petit chou*. I promise.'

Kim stood up, feeling suddenly impatient.

To the Daumier couple, she said, 'It's been lovely meeting you.'

They rose politely; *Madame* kissed Kim's cheeks and her husband kissed her hand with a gallant flourish. '*Au revoir*.'

'*Au revoir*.' She smiled, trying to hide her impatience to get away.

She would have spoken to Simone, but the girl's face was stubbornly set and she refused to meet Kim's eyes.

Kim flushed with embarrassment. Whatever must the French couple be thinking?

She turned irritably to Lawrence. 'Shall we go? The car is some distance away. I only hope I can remember where I left it.'

'So do I,' he said grimly.

With a final '*au revoir*' they left, and Kim didn't dare look back at the faces which looked after them. Two would be full of confused speculation and the other full of hate.

'Why did you do that?' Kim asked, when they were finally in the car and on the road to home.

'Do what?'

His tone wasn't encouraging, but Kim pressed on. 'Leave them like that. You surely weren't in that much of a hurry to get to the telephone.'

He laughed shortly. 'As a matter of fact I was. Once I've decided on something, I like to tie up all the loose ends as soon as possible. That way it's off my mind and I can concentrate on other things.'

She should have left it there, but she somehow felt in a quarrelsome mood.

'In that case, why did you complicate the issue by inviting Simone to lunch in the middle of your negotiations?'

The words came out sounding aggrieved, and he shot her an amused glance.

'As a matter of fact, I did not invite Simone to lunch. She invited herself.'

She took her eyes off the road briefly to look at him.

He raised his brows pointedly. 'Like you, she *just happened to be passing by* at the appropriate moment. But at least she had the courage to announce her arrival. She didn't go scuttling away to hide.'

Kim's face flamed, but she kept her eyes determinedly on the road ahead. 'If you're implying that I was on the spot intentionally, then you're wrong. It would be impossible for me to know where you were, unless I'd followed you. And I had no reason to do that. Besides, I didn't even know you'd left the house.'

'I know.' He sounded happy, and Kim realised he was enjoying listening to her attempts to justify herself.

'You were still tucked up, sleeping blissfully, when I was in the kitchen eating breakfast.'

Kim's insides turned uncomfortably. 'How do you know that?' she gasped. 'Were you. . .spying on me?'

Her blood ran cold. Had he been in her bedroom. . .watching her. . .seeing her at her most defenceless. . .?

'Of course not,' he said calmly. 'I heard your snoring.'

Relief and annoyance in an uncomfortable mixture flooded through her. 'I don't snore. . .' she argued hotly, shooting a furious glance at him.

His face was solemn but his eyes were dancing with mischief. How easy it was for him to bait her, she realised, struggling to get a hold on her temper and the strange riot of sensations he'd deliberately aroused. How could anger be excitement, repulsion be magnetic attraction?

'And if anyone was spying. . .!' he went on goadingly.

'I was not spying.' She knew she shouldn't argue—shouldn't give him the satisfaction of having her explain herself. 'I was going to visit the cathedral. I didn't even know you were in town. I just happened to see you through the window and. . .' She coloured in spite of herself. 'I suppose curiosity got the better of me.'

Curiosity was a good word, she thought a little dizzily. Objective. . .impersonal. . . There could be no confusing it with the warmth of interest.

'I believe you,' he said solemnly. 'But why didn't you come in and announce yourself?'

Kim groaned. 'I don't know. I just felt embarrassed, being seen peering in like that.'

'Quite,' he agreed reasonably. 'But running away was not the solution. Madame Daumier got quite worked up about the mysterious face at the window.'

Kim's toes curled. 'Oh, well!' she said, with an attempt at nonchalance. 'At least she's solved her mystery.' She laughed shortly. 'If two women had turned up in your wake, she would probably have been agog for a week. As it turned out, Simone's initiative was rewarded with lunch, though she would have enjoyed it more if you'd denied all knowledge of me when Madame Daumier pointed me out, and left it at that.' She added in a hard voice which allowed no argument, 'And that's what I intend to do right now. End of discussion.'

CHAPTER SEVEN

ESTELLE was there when they arrived back at the cottage. She was sitting in the garden, relaxing in a lounger with a jug of iced lemonade beside her. She rose as Kim and Lawrence came around the side of the house.

'The kitchen door was open,' she said with an apologetic smile. 'And the garden looked so quiet and peaceful that I decided to wait a while, hoping you would come back.'

She kissed Kim on both cheeks and then reached out to Lawrence for his kiss.

He enveloped her in a huge hug and she pushed him laughingly away. 'Let me look at you.' She surveyed him with satisfaction. 'You are very brown already, Lawrence. It makes you even more handsome.'

She turned teasingly to Kim for confirmation. 'Don't you think so?'

'No comment,' Kim said drily, refusing to meet Lawrence's amused eyes. 'He's conceited enough already.'

Estelle's mouth drooped in disappointment. 'Ah! You are not getting on together?'

Lawrence laughed. 'We rub by,' he said drily. 'But not together. Kim has banished me to the summer-house.'

'I didn't banish you,' Kim denied tightly, annoyed by Estelle's bemused expression. 'You chose to sleep there.'

'And very proper, too,' Estelle said soothingly, obviously trying to pour oil on troubled waters.

She patted Kim's flushed cheek and took her hand in her own elegant one. 'Come! Let's go into the house and have a nice cup of coffee.'

'Good idea,' Lawrence said. 'But not for me, thanks. I have some papers to sort through and then I'll be on the phone for a while.'

He kissed Estelle's cheek. 'I've got some good news, but it'll keep,' he said mysteriously. 'You girls go ahead and enjoy your coffee and a natter. I'll see you later.'

Kim ground her teeth in silent fury. Natter indeed! How dared he? He was doing it deliberately, she knew, but she wasn't fool enough to rise to the bait. Not in front of Estelle, anyway. She would devise a way of retaliating later.

He went off, whistling tunelessly, down to the summer-house.

Estelle laughed, a soft amused sound, and Kim turned to look into her understanding eyes.

'There are times when you hate him, *non*?' She smiled. 'But hate is sometimes as one with love.'

'Not in this case,' Kim said grimly. 'Shall we go in?'

Estelle sat at the table as Kim filled the kettle.

'I've only got instant coffee. Is that all right?'

'Fine.' Estelle relaxed back in her chair. 'You don't mind that I stayed while you were out?' she queried. 'It is so much more peaceful here than at home at the moment.'

'Of course not.' Kim sat beside her to wait for the water to boil, and smelled the faint subtle perfume which always lingered on her skin. Kim suddenly understood why Pamela had spoken of coming home. Estelle had a rare gift for making you feel that you mattered.

'I'm delighted you stayed. You're the first person I've seen in days. And, while I quite enjoy my own company, you can have too much of a good thing.'

Estelle laughed. 'I am having the opposite problem. Too much company. . .not enough solitude. To have a large family is wonderful, but not perhaps when they all come at once to visit.' She sighed. 'But Sunday is the last day, and then my remaining guests will all leave for home and I shall have peace again.'

Some of the family had prolonged their stay for a little holiday and it was obviously becoming a bit of a trial.

The kettle boiled and Kim got up to make the coffee. 'Shall we take it into the living-room?' she asked.

'If you wish.'

Kim carried the tray in and put it down on the coffee-table close to the sofa. 'This is such a lovely room,' she said wistfully, as Estelle settled herself beside her. 'In fact, I love the whole house. I shall miss it when I go home.'

'Yes. I have always loved it too.' She settled back, a faraway look in her eyes. 'Paul and I came to live at the cottage when we were first married. . .before his parents died and we took over the big house.' She sighed. 'We were so happy here. And I always hoped that eventually Georges would bring his bride to live here too. But he and Pamela have plans of their own and that, perhaps, is how it should be.'

'The house belongs to you?' Kim queried faintly. 'Pamela didn't tell me that.'

Estelle laughed. 'Pamela had other things on her mind, I suspect. And who can blame her?'

Kim smiled. 'Yes, who indeed?'

'It was the cottage that first brought them together. I am sure fate intended it to be so. Paul sent Georges to pick Pamela up from the airport and. . .boom. . .' She made an explosive gesture with her hand. 'It all began.'

She smiled mistily. 'It was love at first sight. And now my son is happy and I have a beautiful daughter-in-law.'

She patted Kim's arm affectionately. 'I hope things turn out as well for you, my dear.'

'Thank you.'

Kim wished they would too, but, at the moment, life seemed nothing but frustration. It seemed very unlikely that fate would work the same miracle of love at first sight for her. True, Lawrence Cory had gate-crashed into her life, but it had been more a case of hate at first sight. And, whatever Estelle might believe about hate's being akin to love, it was very far from the truth where she was concerned.

Estelle poured herself another cup of coffee from the pot.

'Ah!' she said, with a little flutter of her elegant fingers. 'I have almost forgotten why I came here to see you.'

She sipped delicately from her cup before going on. 'I thought we should have a little farewell party on Saturday for my departing family and also as a belated birthday surprise for Lawrence.'

'Oh!' Kim was taken by surprise. 'You know it was his birthday recently?'

'But of course! The third of June. He is a Gemini. Clever, intelligent, elusive and so very sexy, *non*?' Estelle's eyes held a wicked gleam. 'Some young woman is going to be *verry* lucky.'

Kim laughed to hide the sudden, inexplicable acceleration of her heartbeat. 'I can see why Pamela loves you so much. You obviously share her interest in astrology.'

'But certainly!' Estelle sounded surprised. 'Doesn't everybody?' She smiled. 'What sign are you, my dear?'

'Virgo!' Kim supplied, a little warily.

'Ah!' Estelle studied Kim's face. 'Not ideal, perhaps, but interesting.'

The cryptic statement aroused Kim's curiosity, but she forbore to ask its meaning. She had a feeling she wouldn't want to hear the answer. 'You're obviously very fond of Lawrence,' she said, by way of changing the subject. She didn't add that she couldn't think why.

'Lawrence and my son have been friends for years,' Estelle said. 'He came here a lot with Georges for the holidays and has become almost like a second son. I love him dearly.' She sighed. 'I only wish he would decide to settle here. . .and find a good wife.'

Kim bit her lip. Estelle was obviously thinking of Simone. If Lawrence was to marry her niece, he would become her nephew. . .and a real member of the family. It was obvious that a liaison between the two would make Estelle very happy indeed.

She wondered, a little sourly, what Simone's star sign might be, and whether Estelle would find that any more ideal.

'I wonder what news Lawrence has to tell me.' Estelle's eyes gleamed with anticipation. 'It is just like him to keep me in suspense.'

Kim was tempted to tell her that Lawrence had decided to buy the Daumier business and stay, but held her tongue. He had mentioned he had good news probably as a primer, and was obviously looking forward to seeing Estelle's face when he told her he would be making his home in France.

It wasn't her business to interfere by letting the

proverbial cat out of the bag, she mused. Soon, she would leave to go home, and they would all carry on their lives without her.

A peculiar feeling of emptiness took Kim by surprise at the thought of going home, leaving the cottage and Estelle. She had a sneaking feeling she would even miss the aggravation that was Lawrence Cory. Which was ridiculous, since she'd hardly had time to get to know them.

Absurdly, her business of Harris Engineering and her impressive office, which had until recently been her entire life, seemed to have faded into the background like a dream. With a start of shocked surprise, she realised that she had given it barely a thought since the day she'd left home.

Lawrence came just as they were finishing their second cup of coffee.

'Lawrence!' Estelle exclaimed sternly. 'What is this exciting news? You must tell me at once.'

'I was going to wait until it was all tied up, legal and watertight,' he said to Estelle, his face wreathed in a wide smile. 'But, since you've twisted my arm, I'll let you into my little secret now. I've bought the Daumier's architectural business in the town. It will be all mine in about a month.'

Estelle squeaked with delight and jumped up excitedly to hug him. 'Oh! I am so pleased! And Georges will be delighted. He was so hoping you would decide that way.' She beamed, looking up at him slyly from beneath her lashes.

'All you will need now is the right girl to marry you and to give you a family.' She reached up and pinched his cheek.

Kim stifled a gasp at this rather obvious pleading of

Simone's cause. Did Lawrence realise where this conversation was leading? Obviously not! She had half expected him to be annoyed at this blatant piece of female manipulation, but he only laughed.

'And I suppose you have a suitable wife already selected for me?'

'But of course.' Estelle smiled demurely. 'You don't believe I would allow you to make such a choice alone, do you?'

'On reflection, no!' He bent to kiss her nose, a half-serious frown between his dark brows. 'But, in the end, you know that I will.'

'We shall see,' she said mysteriously.

'Is that the reason you came?' Lawrence asked teasingly. 'To tell me you had turned marriage broker?'

'*Mais non!* I came to tell you that the family is having a little farewell party on Saturday.' She smiled happily. 'Now we have your news, of course, it will become a special celebration.'

She didn't mention his birthday, but shot Kim a conspiratorial little wink. 'I too have a little surprise up my sleeve. But you will have to wait until Saturday to hear it.'

'You always were a heartless woman.'

'How could it be otherwise. . .when you have my heart?' She stood up to kiss him on both cheeks. 'But now it is time I went.'

She kissed Kim and said to Lawrence, 'Look after Kimberley and I look forward to seeing you both on Saturday.'

Lawrence shot a wicked glance at Kim. 'I'd be very happy to look after Kimberley, if she'd only let me.'

The message in his smiling eyes sent hot colour rushing to her cheeks. How dared he flirt with her in this outrageous way in front of Estelle?

She glared at him. 'I can take care of myself, thanks.'

Estelle laughed, and touched Kim's temper-flushed cheek. 'You must not mind him, *chérie*. He is a true Gemini, impulsive, demanding. He does not understand your cautious heart.'

She stretched up and pinched Lawrence's cheek. 'You must learn patience, *mon chou*. You will find easier signs to conquer than Miss Virgo.'

He laughed. 'Thanks. I'll bear that in mind.'

A clear warning to keep off the grass, Kim thought wryly. Whether Lawrence realised it or not, Estelle was already subtly manipulating him.

Lawrence came into the kitchen after Estelle had gone and sat down at the table. 'I wouldn't mind that cup of coffee now,' he said.

Kim had her back to him—she was boiling the kettle—but she could feel his gaze on her, filling her with uncomfortable heat. She would have liked to tell him to get his own coffee, but restrained herself. It was hard to say why she felt so irritable around him, but it seemed always to be that way.

Without answering, she made two cups of coffee and handed him one, hesitating before sitting at the table with her own cup.

'Do I detect a touch of frost?' he asked cheerfully.

Kim laughed grimly. 'I'd be surprised if you did. A rhinoceros hide is hardly that sensitive.'

'I don't suppose it is, but you manage to pierce mine easily enough with your expert little darts.'

'But not enough to penetrate your ego,' she snapped back.

Unexpectedly, he reached across the table and captured her hand, turning the palm upwards to place a kiss in the centre, closing her fingers over it.

'A gesture of peace.' His eyes smiled teasingly into hers. 'Today's a special day for me, so why don't we mark the occasion by calling a truce?'

Kim felt an unwilling urge to smile into his compelling eyes, but stifled it. 'We're not at war,' she said stiffly, pulling her hand from his.

'Aren't we?' His face grew softly serious. 'You could have fooled me.'

Caught by his gaze, Kim felt the magnetic pull of his vitality. Why was it so easy for him to demolish her defences?

'I can't help what you feel,' she said defensively.

His mouth curved ironically. 'Unfortunately, neither can I.'

His gaze, probing hers, seemed to give the words special meaning, and Kim's eyes widened in automatic response to the unspoken appeal, leaving her speechless.

The next moment she was doubting her senses, as his mood changed abruptly.

'If you'll excuse me, I have one or two more phone calls to make. Perhaps I'll see you later.'

His offhand assumption had her bristling all over again.

She didn't see him again until the evening. She'd been sitting in the living-room, trying to read a book, but the words danced meaninglessly before her eyes. She still felt wound-up and irritable and couldn't help wishing she had a little company. Even Lawrence Cory would have been welcome at the moment.

Now they'd called a truce, it might be possible for them to hold a conversation that wasn't punctuated by annoying skirmishes.

At nine o'clock, she got her wish. He turned up, carrying a bottle of champagne and two glasses.

'I thought you might like to help me celebrate a major turning-point in my life. It's not every day a man decides to change the country of his abode.'

Without protest, Kim took the glass he offered.

'I'll drink to that.' She lifted her glass and swallowed the cool, dry liquid. 'Here's to success. . .and. . . happiness,' she toasted him, after a little hesitation in which she silently argued whether happiness would be what he'd find with Simone.

'To success. . .and happiness,' he repeated, and took a long swallow of champagne before sitting down beside Kim on the sofa and refilling her glass.

Kim felt the drink warming her insides and would have felt more relaxed if he hadn't been so close. His nearness made her nervous, and she swallowed down the last of her champagne and put her empty glass down on the little table.

'Do you think you'll enjoy living in France?' she asked conversationally.

'I know I will,' he said. 'Everything I want is here. Given certain circumstances, I could be very happy.' He looked directly at her. 'How about you?'

'Oh, yes! I think so!' Caught in his incredible amber gaze, Kim was suddenly breathless, but she pressed on determinedly. 'Of course, my circumstances differ from yours. I have a business that isn't transportable, but if I were to choose to live anywhere other than where I do, it would be here. It's so lovely.'

'I agree.' His voice was softly husky, and Kim dropped her head, unable to go on meeting his eyes without flushing at what she saw there.

His arm was along the back of the sofa, close to her face, and his long fingers idly brushed a strand of hair from her cheek.

'*You're* lovely, Kim,' he said softly, and slowly he

leaned towards her so that his face was close to hers. 'I don't think you know how lovely.'

She could feel his breath against her cheek, smell the tangy scent of his aftershave, and his lips, so close to hers, had her teetering on the brink of an abyss.

Unconsciously inviting, her chin lifted and her lids began to droop, and he lowered his head to bring his lips to hers.

She heard him sigh and answered him with a sigh of her own as she felt the warm pressure of his mouth against hers, gently exploring, promising so much, demanding only that she meet him halfway. She was tempted. . .terribly tempted. . .but some small, sane corner of her mind was still alert to the temptation and the consequences.

Slowly, she pulled back, looking into his face, searching for the mockery she feared would be there, but he was gently shaking his head.

'Sweet coward,' he said.

He leaned across to the radio and turned it on to a channel playing romantic music.

'A little background magic,' he murmured, and stood up, drawing her to her feet. 'Let's dance.'

Somehow, it was impossible to resist him, and as his arms closed about her she moved into his embrace, lifting her cheek to his.

There's no harm in this, she told herself a little desperately, but the brush of his body against hers as they moved to the slow rhythm was sheer torment and there was no mistaking the mounting excitement in him.

He released her hand from his and placed it against his chest, where it slid slowly up around his neck as she nestled closer. The most undreamt-of sensations were making themselves felt in her as his arms tightened and his hands moved gently against her back.

Her lips burned in anticipation, but he didn't kiss her. The frustration was unbearable, the suffering exquisite, forcing an exasperated cry.

He heard the almost inaudible sound and moved back a little, his brilliant eyes probing her own, which were wide and defenceless as she stared back at him.

He drew her back into his arms, his hand tangling in the thick hair at the nape of her neck, his mouth covering hers with a sudden possessive force that shocked her into response. She'd been a fool to think there was no harm in this. . .but the harm was from the surging sensations of her own body as it strained against his.

The music had stopped now and a man was speaking in swift, unintelligible French, but still he held her gathered against him, her breasts crushed against the hardness of him as his kiss deepened. . .lengthened. . .

The telephone's ringing startled them both and Kim jumped back, her heart pounding against her ribs. The back of her legs touched against the sofa and she almost fell down into its softness, panting as though she'd been running a race.

'Damn!' Lawrence cursed, and Kim could see that his hand was shaking as he lifted the receiver.

'Who the hell. . .?' His voice was ragged with annoyance. 'What. . .?'

A dark frown settled on his brow as he thrust the receiver towards Kim. 'It's for you.'

'Who. . .?' she asked in a tremulous voice, but he turned away without answering.

'Kim, is that you?' Charles's voice came irritably down the line. 'Who was that?'

'Lawrence Cory,' Kim said, trying to calm her agitated nerves.

'What's he doing there with you at this time of night?' Charles demanded belligerently, and Kim, now cold and shaken, felt tempted to tell him to mind his own bloody business. It was bad enough to have one man's reducing her to a quivering wreck without another playing the outraged suitor.

'We're celebrating,' she answered shortly. 'As you say, it's quite late. Did you want something important?'

'I called to say I was missing you, but it's obvious you aren't missing me.' Charles's hurt voice only added to her irritation. 'What are you celebrating? Is it a party?'

Kim's eyes went to Lawrence Cory, who was standing at the window staring out at the stars with an air of suppressed fury about him. If it was a party, he wasn't enjoying it, she thought, smothering a reckless giggle.

'Not exactly,' she said into the phone. 'And if you've rung me to conduct the Spanish Inquisition, I think I'll ring off.'

'I'm sorry,' Charles said, sounding flustered. 'But surely I must have some right to——'

'No right at all, Charles,' Kim cut in furiously. 'And the last thing I need is a minder. Now, if you don't mind, I'm rather tired, so I'll say goodnight.' She slammed the receiver into its rest, staring at it sightlessly as she battled to restore her ragged breathing to normal.

When she looked in his direction again, Lawrence Cory was sitting on the window-ledge, his long legs stretched out in front of him and a thoughtful expression on his face.

'If you say anything at all,' she flared, 'I'll. . . I'll throw you out.'

'And, in your present mood, I'll bet you could do it.' He smiled mockingly. 'And I was only going to say congratulations. . .'

Kim picked up the first thing that came to hand and aimed it at him. Fortunately, the empty glass fell short of his head as he moved hastily for the door.

He was in the bathroom the following morning, shaving.

He'd left the door open and Kim went in, already unwrapping her dressing-gown to get into the shower.

She gasped when she saw him there, and drew the robe about her in embarrassment.

He grinned. 'Don't worry, you have no secrets from me. I have a photographic memory.'

Kim stared at him coldly. 'You're on shameless form again this morning, I notice.'

Deliberately mistaking her meaning, he looked down at his bare chest and the muscled legs revealed by a pair of skimpy shorts.

Kim's eyes had followed his, taking in the male beauty of him, aware of a deep, strange ache inside. She tore her gaze away as he laughed.

'Thanks. But I reckon you win on points for shape.'

Kim blushed at his open appraisal, but was secretly glad he was back to sparring with her. It would have been impossible otherwise to stand the embarrassment of last night. She'd been angry at Charles, but had since had time to reflect and silently thank him for his timely interruption which had saved her from her champagne-induced idiocy.

'Are you going to be here all day?' she asked sharply.

'Not all day,' he said pleasantly. 'Actually, I was thinking of taking a boat up-river. Do you fancy coming?'

Kim felt the leap of her heart with a surge of self-disgust. 'I don't think so.'

'It'll be cool there, with some wonderful scenery.'

The warm look in his eyes signalled danger and yet still she was tempted. This stupidity has to stop, she admonished herself. You are skating on very thin ice.

'Thanks. But I'm expecting a telephone call.'

His smile disappeared, to be replaced by a frown. 'From lover-boy? Are you planning to apologise?'

'Charles is not my lover-boy,' she bit back, infuriated by his stinging mockery. 'And I have nothing to apologise for. . .to anyone.'

'Good.' He was grinning again. 'He's not your type anyway.'

'Thanks. You've already expressed that opinion.'

He nodded. 'But I know you better now, and I'm convinced he isn't your Mr Right.'

'Do you suppose you are?' she shot back angrily.

'Perhaps,' he said, adding to her frustration. 'I'm waiting for you to make up your mind on that point.'

'If and when I do I'll let you know,' she said bitingly. 'But I don't think I'll be wasting much time on the subject.'

He was calmly splashing cold water on his face and wiping it on a hand towel, ignoring the angry rise and fall of her breast as she struggled with the remnants of her anger.

'I ought to just let you stew in your own sour juices,' he said, as he splashed on a little aftershave. 'But instead, I'll give you one last chance to add a little enjoyment to your holiday.'

Kim watched, with unwilling fascination, the play of his muscles as he pulled a clean T-shirt over his head, and wondered why she didn't just turn away and go.

'Monsieur Daumier has loaned me his little cabin

cruiser for the day and I'll be ready to go in half an hour. Don't worry about breakfast, I've already packed a hamper.'

He leaned to kiss her cheek. 'And that's as close as I'll get to you all day, I promise.' His amber eyes danced. 'If that's the way you want it.'

In the shower, Kim battled with her pride. Why should she allow him to ride roughshod over her like this? He thought that all he had to do was snap his fingers and she would come running. On the other hand, the prospect of a day on the river was very appealing and, as he'd said, why shouldn't she add a little enjoyment to her holiday with an innocent day out? And innocent it would be, he'd given his word, unless she chose otherwise, and she wasn't likely to do that.

She was ready and waiting for him in the kitchen, a wary expression in her blue eyes as they met his bright amber gaze.

'That's my girl,' he said, with a good-humoured grin.

Kim, grateful that he hadn't crowed over his victory, let the remark pass.

'I half suspect you only asked me to go with you so that I could drive you there,' she said drily, as he walked with her to the car, a picnic basket held easily in the crook of his arm.

'Why else would I have invited you?'

He caught Kim's indignant glare with a grin.

'That's what you wanted to hear, isn't it? And I've promised everything will be the way you want it today.'

And everything, Kim grudgingly had to admit, was just perfect.

As Lawrence had predicted, the morning was already warm under a cloudless sky, and the little cruiser moved smoothly along between the river-banks, delighting Kim with an ever-changing landscape.

'This is wonderful,' she sighed. 'I'm so glad I came.'

'I hate to say it. . .' He cupped her chin with his fingers and dropped a light kiss on her nose '. . .but I told you so.'

Kim, still tingling from his brief caress, nodded her head. 'And you were right.'

His eyes met hers with a friendly little smile that had her pulses jumping as erratically as any smouldering look.

'If you're good,' he said teasingly, 'I'll let you have a go at being captain.'

'Thank you, kind sir,' she answered demurely, and then laughed.

It was a morning of enchantment.

'How is it I've not seen this side of you before?' she asked half-seriously. 'It's so much more relaxing.'

'Perhaps it's because this is the first time you've really looked at the real me, instead of some symbol of whatever spectre haunts you.'

'There isn't any spectre,' she denied quickly, and then stopped at his quizzical look.

'There was someone,' she amended. 'But it was all a long time ago.'

'Want to talk about it?'

She shook her head. 'There's nothing left to talk about now.' With a shock, she realised that it was true. Philip Crossley had lost his power to hurt her. In a moment of unguarded honesty, she said, 'And, though I hate to say it, I have you to thank for that.'

His hands were on her shoulders, his eyes devouring her face as she looked up at him. For a moment, he seemed about to kiss her, and then he pulled away with a sharp little groan.

'I promised hands off and I intend to keep my promise.' He began guiding the boat in towards the bank. 'I think we'll eat our lunch on dry land.'

Kim, still wrestling with an inexplicable surge of disappointment, helped him to tie up and get the picnic things on to the bank.

She laughed as he handed her a fold-up table and two chairs, followed by the hamper, which contained a snowy tablecloth and napkins, as well as food.

'We're really dining in style,' she teased.

'Why not?'

'Why not, indeed?' Kim echoed a little giddily.

'Compliments of Château Baron!' he quipped, as he produced a bottle of wine. 'Nothing but the best.'

Crisp French bread with cold chicken, pâté, cheese and tangy green apples, washed down with the white, faintly sweet wine, made a delicious meal, and Kim sat back at last with a dreamy expression on her face.

'That was perfect,' she said.

Lawrence went to the boat and came back with a thick blanket, which he spread on the grass.

Kim tensed. 'Have I been softened up for seduction?'

He threw two cushions on to the blanket. 'If you can find a man out here in the wilds, go ahead. But I'm about to have a nap.'

He got down on to the blanket and stretched himself out. 'Wake me when you want to go.'

Kim busied herself clearing up the remains of the meal, rinsing the plates and glasses in the river before wiping them and packing them away. When she'd finished, she sat down on the blanket beside Lawrence, peering surreptitiously at his lean, handsome face. His eyes were closed and his breathing was soft and even and it really did look as though he was sleeping.

She took the opportunity to study him more closely,

her eyes following the arch of his brows, the fascinating curve of his strong nose, the sensual lines of his mouth, softened and slightly parted, only looking away as her pulse began to race. Even sleeping, he could rouse her to this unwilling excitement, she thought resentfully. He didn't need to touch her.

Determinedly, she tore her eyes away to the gentle sweep of the field as it rose up the hill. It had been empty when they'd disembarked, but now Kim could see the outline of cows on the horizon. They were moving slowly down, grazing absorbedly. For some reason, Kim felt uneasy. She wasn't afraid of animals, but there seemed an air of menace about one of them in particular, who was bigger than the rest, with large pointed horns, and it was looking intently in her direction.

'Lawrence,' she said, 'wake up.'

The animals seemed to be converging now, drawing together into a tighter group, all of them headed their way, with the large beast at the centre.

Filled with a sudden sense of urgency, she leaned over and shook Lawrence. 'Lawrence, for heaven's sake, wake up! We've got company.'

'What?' He opened drowsy eyes, which cleared immediately at the look of apprehension on her face.

He sat up as the cattle began to run.

'They're probably just curious,' he said. 'But it's better to take no chances.' He stood up. 'Get into the boat. I'll get the stuff.'

'Don't bother with the stuff,' Kim said on a rising note of panic as their visitors drew nearer. 'Just run.'

Ignoring her plea, Lawrence began to fold the chairs and table, and had just picked up the hamper when the bull charged.

Kim screamed a warning and began to run. Lawrence

dropped the hamper, grabbing her hand as he caught up with her. Her feet seemed hardly to touch the ground as they covered the distance to the boat. Lawrence practically threw her over the side on to the small deck before pushing the boat away from the bank and then clambering on board, drenched to the skin.

The bull was staring at them from the bank.

'He looks positively disappointed,' Kim said shakily, a little ashamed now of her moment of panic.

'He's probably quite harmless.' Lawrence laughed grimly. 'But I think we were wise not to wait to find out.'

'What shall we do about the things we've left behind?' Kim asked a little anxiously. 'I don't suppose the Daumiers will be pleased to lose their deck furniture.'

'I'll pick it up later, when our friends have lost interest and gone back over the hill,' Lawrence reassured her. 'But first, let's get out of these wet clothes.'

Kim looked down at her mud-spattered shorts. 'I'm not so much wet as dirty,' she said ruefully. 'But you're wringing wet. We'll have to turn back.'

'No problem,' he said, and, before Kim's horrified gaze, he stripped off his shirt and began unzipping his shorts. He laughed as she turned hastily away. 'Don't worry about preserving your modesty. I'm wearing swimming trunks.'

'Well, at least that's something,' Kim said, trying to stem the rise of colour to her cheeks. Even his trunks left little to the imagination. She busied herself picking up his wet clothes and draping them on the roof of the cockpit. 'With a bit of luck, these will dry in the sun.'

The brief excitement seemed to have drawn them closer together, and the rest of the afternoon passed pleasurably. They reached a weir further up-river and, rather than take the diversion, they turned around and headed back. The cows had disappeared from the field where they'd picnicked and Lawrence was able to retrieve their belongings without any further trouble.

Back at the cottage, Kim was half tempted to ask Lawrence to have supper, but, relaxed and happy, she suspected there was a good chance she might make a fool of herself. All day, on the river, she'd been conscious of his charisma, and had more than once been tempted to touch him, but knew it would be unwise. He'd kept his promise to keep his distance and Kim had been relieved, but conscious of an underlying disappointment. What do you want from the poor man? she mentally castigated herself, knowing that if he'd even so much as tried to kiss her she would have blamed him bitterly. And now, here she was, on the verge of issuing him with an invitation to a cosy little supper which might lead them anywhere.

He solved her dilemma, however.

'If you don't mind, I'll leave you now. I've got some work to do on the designs for Georges's and Pamela's house. I'm seeing the builders there tomorrow.'

'OK.' Kim didn't argue. 'Well, thanks for a lovely day. I've enjoyed every minute.'

'Not half as much as I did.' It was growing dusk and his eyes gleamed as bright as flames in the half-light. 'Am I allowed a goodnight kiss?'

Kim's heart leapt, but she nodded coolly enough.

He moved closer, his hand slipping beneath her hair to the sensitive nape of her neck, and slowly he drew her lips to his in a light, sweet kiss that had Kim tingling from her head to her toes.

When finally he lifted his head, Kim wondered what he'd seen in her face to make him smile in that heart-stopping way.

CHAPTER EIGHT

KIM didn't see Lawrence the following morning, and she assumed he'd gone off early to keep his appointment with the builders.

Feeling strangely restless, she prowled the garden, noting that the grass needed cutting and the hedges were crying out for the attentions of a clipper. She was tempted to look in the sheds, tucked away at the entrance to the wood, for some gardening tools to improve matters, but the project was daunting, even in her present state of pent-up energy.

Perhaps she should just mention it to Estelle at the party, since the house and grounds were her property.

It had come as a shock to know that the cottage belonged to the Baron family. Somehow she had never connected the two. But now, of course, it made sense. No wonder Pamela had felt obliged to let Lawrence Cory stay.

She wondered, not for the first time, what surprise Estelle had in store for Lawrence. A birthday surprise obviously, but Kim had a feeling it would be something a little more momentous than that. Estelle had been quite open about her hopes for Lawrence's future. She hadn't been quite as open about her probable plans for Simone, but Kim had a sneaking suspicion that the two went hand in glove.

And if Simone had anything to do with it, Kim mused grimly, that was precisely how it would be.

On the bank of the stream, Kim came across her discarded T-shirt and shorts from days ago, lying grubby and still damp. She picked them up, remembering, with a rush of colour to her throat, how Lawrence had hauled her naked out of the stream. The memory was closely followed by a picture which seared across her inner eye. Lawrence, towering above her, his powerful body gleaming with water. He'd been naked too, but had obviously felt no shame.

Kim closed her eyes and swallowed convulsively, recalling vividly the sensations of her body against his as he'd carried her to the house. . .feeling again the heated tremors of excitement which had burned through her. . .

She shook herself out of it, unnerved by the strength of the memory, and began to make her way back to the house. She'd make a reviving cup of coffee and then take a stroll down to the village. Hanging around the house alone was definitely something to be avoided today.

On the way back, she paused at the summer-house, filled with a sudden overwhelming curiosity. She had never actually been inside the little wooden building. . .never even so much as peered through the window. Once Lawrence had established himself there, the place had seemed to be his domain. . .too personal. . .too intimate. . .to explore.

But now, questions rose which she simply couldn't leave unanswered. Where did he sleep? What did he do with his time there?

She told herself it was none of her business, but knew she was going to go inside anyway.

The interior was a shock. The place was positively luxurious. The floor was inlaid wood-blocks, graded and arranged to form intricate patterns, and the walls were lined with bleached pine which reflected the light and made the place bright and airy. Thick woollen rugs were scattered about, the clear bright colours echoed in the curtains and the hand-woven bedspread on the deep and comfortable day-bed tucked away in a windowed recess. Wooden cupboards lined one wall and there was an oval dining table and chairs. Tucked away in another recess was a sink unit and a small, two-ringed stove. There was also a shower cubicle and separate toilet in a small rear lobby. Kim gasped. The place had everything he needed and there really hadn't been any need for him to use the house. So why had he done so, if not just to irritate. . .or perhaps seduce her?

Artist's paraphernalia was scattered about—pots with assortments of brushes, boxes containing tubes of oil-paints. Two easels had been set up with canvases, one with a half-finished view of the old mill, the other covered with a cloth.

Kim stood before it and bit her lip. He'd told her once before that he hated people to see his work half finished and something told her he would be furious at anyone who unveiled this canvas for a sneak preview. But he wasn't here, an insistent little inner voice prompted, so he would never know.

With hands that shook slightly, she carefully removed the cloth and then almost dropped it from fingers that had suddenly become nerveless.

Her own face peered out at her, glowing with excitement.

She was sitting on the ledge in the stream, her unclothed body gleaming wetly, her legs and thighs barely concealed by the clear water. But it was the expression on her face which set her heart pounding furiously. Her lips were softly parted, her eyes large and wide with a kind of breathless anticipation, as she gazed upwards. No one else seeing the picture would know what it was she was looking at with such wrapt attention. But Kim knew and so did Lawrence Cory.

White with shock and growing anger, Kim stared at the picture. The thing was an obvious mockery, designed purely to humiliate her. Yesterday, on the river, she had thought she'd got close to the real Lawrence, and the feeling of friendly warmth had remained with her until now. But the more she looked at the portrait, the more she became convinced that everything, even yesterday, had been part of a preconceived plan to conquer her for the sake of his own ego.

For long moments, she fought with an urge to destroy the painting, to tear it to shreds, the way she had the sketch he'd done of her in the field, but something warned her it would be a dangerous thing to do.

But if she didn't it would exist as some kind of malicious visual exposure of feelings she didn't understand and which she would far rather forget. She gave a shudder of revulsion.

'Is it that bad?'

The voice, speaking so close to her ear, startled her heart into a painful hammering which left her breathless and rocking on her feet. Turning quickly to face him, she almost lost her balance, but he made no effort to steady her. He stood with his hands thrust into the pockets of his light trousers, surveying her through eyes that were cool and unreadable.

'It's worse than bad.' Kim found her voice in an eruption of fury. 'It's insulting. . .humiliating. . .'

She ran out of adjectives to express her feelings and stepped forward instead to lash out, pummelling her fists against his hard chest in a fury of frustration.

He caught her wrists easily, his fingers strong and tensile against the delicate bones.

'Calm down,' he said tautly. 'And take another look.'

Adroitly, he turned her so that her back was against him, his arms encircling her, holding her prisoner within a steely grip. 'Now what do you see?'

Kim was tempted to shut her eyes tight, but, with a feeling of almost morbid fascination, she confronted the portrait. But her churning senses denied its revelation.

'What am I supposed to see?' she asked woodenly.

He sighed and gave her an exasperated shake. 'Would it help if I told you what I intend to call the painting? Its title?'

He paused, but Kim maintained a stubborn, helpless silence.

'I've called it "Birth of Desire".'

'"Birth of. . .?"' Kim's face flamed.

'Go on!' he prompted. 'Say it. *Desire*.'

His mouth brushed her cheek slowly, persuasively, making her almost cry out.

'You didn't invent the feeling, Kim.' His voice was softly amused. 'It comes as part of the kit. We all have it. . .in some degree or another.'

She struggled against him, but he held her tight within the circle of his arms.

She squirmed inwardly at his deliberate taunting. He'd brought her face to face with what she had been hiding from herself. . .with what had been there almost from the start. . .and she hated him for it.

'You really do think you're clever, don't you?' she accused bitterly.

He turned her suddenly to face him, his hold just as steely. . .just as impossible to break. . .and his eyes glowed intently into hers.

'Clever enough to know you want me,' he said.

'What I can't work out is why you think that's so terrible.'

'You're entitled to your opinion,' Kim said, sounding calm, but feeling desperate. 'It doesn't have to be right.'

'Agreed,' he said reasonably. 'But I think a number of people might agree with me, once they've seen that portrait.'

Kim's eyes widened in horror. 'You wouldn't dare!' she spat disgustedly, and then gasped, as an even worse thought occurred to her. 'Do you mean. . .you intend. . .you're going to exhibit it. . .sell it. . .?'

He lifted broad shoulders in a shrug. 'I might. It's good and should fetch quite a bit.' He laughed shortly. 'On the other hand, I may decide to give it to you. . .to remind you of what might have been.'

Kim's wavering control suddenly snapped. 'Why you. . .conceited. . .!' Her voice was almost a sob.

'What has conceit to do with it?' he taunted.

Sick humiliation flooded through her and she struggled to be free of his hold, but he kept her tightly within his arms.

'Desire,' he whispered, pressing his lips against her ear, sending strange shafts of sensation shooting up her spine. 'It's what was in your eyes when you looked at me that day by the stream. It's in your eyes now. . .behind the fear. . .'

'No!' The word was torn from Kim's oddly tight throat.

His hand thrust into the thick hair, forcing her face up, his eyes probing hers mercilessly.

'Liar!' he said, his voice unnervingly soft. 'You want me and we both know it.'

'It's not true!' Kim denied, in a voice that shook.

'Isn't it?'

In a sudden movement, his lips covered hers in a brief, searing kiss which had her already shaken senses spinning dizzily.

It was over in a flash, and he smiled at her.

'You wouldn't want to bet on that?'

Without waiting for her answer, he lifted her up and carried her across to the day-bed in the recess. Almost roughly, he deposited her there and stood back. Before her horrified gaze, he began to strip, removing his shirt swiftly before unbuckling the belt of his trousers.

'Lawrence! For heaven's sake!' she pleaded, her breath strangely restricted in her dry throat.

'Patience, my little love,' he mocked, his amber eyes gleaming softly. 'I'll be with you soon.'

'That's not what I meant!' she wailed, but he only smiled.

Slipping deftly out of his trousers and pants, he stood before her, towering over her as he had at the stream, his powerful body bronzed and gleaming. . .and obviously aroused.

'See!' he said, gently mocking. 'I can't get away with denying I want you.'

Kim's mouth dropped open. Rendered speechless by the strength of the unfamiliar feelings that set her alight and churned at her insides, she licked at her dry lips, wishing she could turn away, but powerless to do anything but go on looking.

'And now the portrait has come to life.' His smile was exultant. 'Say you want me,' he commanded tautly. 'Tell me!'

He was beautiful and she was overwhelmed by an urge to touch him, a realisation which brought hot, shameful colour flooding to her cheeks.

'Stop this!' she cried in a strangled voice, able at last to put her hands to her eyes and drop her head.

He was there beside her, pulling her hands away, leaving her no place to hide from his probing gaze.

'I said I'd wait until you wanted me,' he reminded her softly, brushing his lips against her burning mouth. 'Now I think the waiting's over.'

He was releasing the buttons of her blouse, sweeping it gently from her shoulders, revealing the firm swelling breasts, his amber eyes alight with a kind of delight.

Gently, he pushed her back on to the bed, and she seemed powerless to stop him as he eased off her shorts and pants.

Coherent thought seemed impossible. He was right. She wanted him and the knowledge had her burning with shame.

He kissed her deeply, his mouth devouring hers, his body poised against hers, demanding her surrender.

She was on the edge of a precipice, teetering, trembling. . .

He lifted his lips to murmur raggedly, 'You can stop me now.'

Kim shuddered. He was offering her an escape from this exquisite torture. All she had to do was speak.

His hands caressed her to fever-pitch, driving her closer to the edge.

'Kim.' He murmured her name against her lips, releasing, as though by some magic incantation, the crumbling barriers of restraint.

She groaned, a sound of sweet defeat, and, as he moved to possess her, her body merged exultantly with his in an undreamt-of surge of ecstacy.

Kim lay beside Lawrence, the aftermath of his loving still reverberating through her sensitised body.

He'd held her for a long time afterwards, his hand stroking her hair and down her spine, his lips against her forehead, but now he was sleeping, his sensuous lips parted, his breathing light and peaceful.

Gently, she turned on her side, coming up on one elbow so that she could look at him more closely.

Loving her, he had seemed all-powerful. . . undeniable. . .and she had delivered herself wholly to him without counting the cost. Asleep, he looked younger and strangely vulnerable, and there was a peculiar ache inside her. Her fingers itched to stroke his lean cheek, but she didn't want to wake him. She needed time to think, time to adjust to the changes he had brought about, before she could face him again.

Carefully, she eased herself off the bed, reclaiming her discarded clothing with hands that shook as memories of how he had removed them threatened to engulf her.

He's won his bet, she thought, in an attempt at cynicism, amazed to find it didn't matter.

He'd got her to admit she could desire him and, later, she would undoubtedly feel the humiliation of that. But, for now, she was filled with a feeling of warmth which had nothing to do with the heat of the day.

She was in the kitchen, drinking tea, still trying to come to terms with her confusing contentment, when he appeared at the door, barefoot and wearing only his trousers.

'Is there another cup in the pot?' he asked.

Kim shot him a shy look, shaken by the frown on his unexpectedly subdued face.

'Yes. I'll pour you one.'

'Don't bother. I can help myself.'

He looked pale, she thought, and wished she had the courage to touch him.

'Are you all right?' he asked, sounding unexpectedly anxious.

She smiled, wanting to see him grin, but his face was guarded. Oh, God! she thought with sudden horror, he's regretting it!

It was something she hadn't bargained for, and it cut through her euphoria like a knife.

He sat opposite her at the table, sipping at his tea reflectively for a long time without speaking.

Kim waited in an agony of suspense, but unable to break the silence.

'Kim,' he said at last, 'I'm sorry. It should never have happened. It was just that you——'

Kim felt a sense of panic.

'Oh, please!' she cut in, unable to listen to whatever explanation he was about to give. He'd made love to her and now he was wishing that he hadn't and that was unbearable. 'Please don't explain.'

He gripped her hand, capturing it against the table. His expression was grim. 'I didn't know it was your first time. If I had. . .' He stopped and shook his head.

'If you had. . .?' Kim prompted him, surprised at the steadiness of her voice.

'I would never have. . .' A grimace of apparent pain worked his features.

'You would never have taken on the responsibility. . .' Kim continued for him as her anger grew '. . .of being first with a virgin.'

His grip on her hand tightened, almost crushing her bones. 'Stop it, Kim!' he cried fiercely, his amber eyes burning into her cool blue ones.

Kim's laugh cut him dead. To her own ears it sounded faintly hysterical, but her voice was calm.

'There's no need to feel guilty,' she said tersely. 'I'm grateful to you. Virginity in a woman of my age can be a positive handicap. From now on, things will be easier.'

'Cheap,' he cut in icily. 'Kimberley! That was cheap!'

'It wasn't meant to be. As it happens, I'm just speaking the truth. You've provided me with a valuable experience.'

'Thanks.' Lawrence's eyes bored into hers. 'I'm glad I could help.'

She managed a smile. 'You'll never know how much.'

She drained her cup and stood up. If she didn't leave now, she might begin to cry.

'If you'll excuse me, I think I'd like to have a bath.'

CHAPTER NINE

KIM was sitting in the garden under the shade of the broad-leaf tree, her eyes closed against the light as she tried to decide what she would wear to Estelle's party.

Choosing wouldn't be easy. The wardrobe she'd brought with her wasn't extensive and she hadn't thought to ask Estelle whether the gathering would be formal or informal.

She was tempted to wear the midnight-blue dress again, but Lawrence had already seen that at the hotel. Not that that mattered, she assured herself, but she was in a mood for making the most of her appearance. She had no interest in competing with Simone for his attention, of course, but that didn't mean she had to look like an English mouse.

A shadow fell across her, making her start, and she opened her eyes to find Lawrence looking down at her, a wary expression on his lean tanned face.

'Did I wake you?'

He sat down in a garden chair beside her and helped himself to a glass of lemonade.

'I wasn't sleeping.' Kim was uncomfortably aware of him in his skimpy shorts, his bare, gleaming skin a reminder of feelings she'd been trying to forget. 'I was thinking about the party tonight.'

He nodded. 'So, you still intend to go?'

She stared at him. Was he trying to put her off the idea? 'Of course! Is there any reason why I shouldn't?'

'None at all,' he said, with a shrug that accused her

of over-reacting. 'I just wanted to know your intentions. Since you're going, perhaps you'd give me a lift.'

Kim smiled coolly. 'We seem to be back to square one.'

He nodded. 'So it seems. Once this business is settled I'll be investing in a car of my own, but for now I'm reliant on your unfailing good nature.'

There was a gleam in his eye that warned her he was back to teasing.

'If that's a crack,' she said, 'it's no way to get yourself a lift.'

His brows rose subtly. 'Would coaxing be a better way?'

He reached for her hand, but she evaded him.

'No, it wouldn't.' Her face flamed. 'You can't win your way always by coercion.'

His face was suddenly still. 'I didn't coerce you, Kim, and you know it.'

Kim laughed unpleasantly. 'Would you feel better if you could believe that?'

'I just wish I'd known the name of the game. How was I to know you'd never——?' He broke off and looked at her closely, a lowering frown between his brows. 'You were thinking of going into marriage with lover-boy, having had no sexual experience at all?'

He shook his head disbelievingly, and Kim felt her hackles rise.

'It might be the axis of the world to you,' she bit back, 'but in my opinion there's a lot more to a relationship than sex.'

He nodded. 'True. But how ever little or much there is of it in a relationship, sex has got to work, or the rest doesn't. Don't you agree?'

Kim took a sharp inward breath. Until he'd made love to her, she had thought all men were like Philip

Crossley, harsh, careless, selfish. . .capable of arousing in her only an icy desolation. And yet, at the time, she had thought she'd loved Philip.

And, as both Pamela and Lawrence Cory had pointed out, marriage to Charles had been intended as a compromise, a halfway-house between spinsterhood and marriage. A comfortable, undemanding companionship that would fit in easily with the organised kind of life she had planned.

'Do you think we could drop this discussion?' she said coldly. 'Unfortunately, it doesn't hold the same fascination for me as it does for you.'

His lips curved cynically. 'That wasn't my impression.'

Kim's face flamed. He obviously had no intention of sparing her feelings. 'I might have expected you to crow,' she said through clenched teeth, 'but I didn't think even you would sink that low.'

Her furious eyes met his in a challenge, but he was shaking his head. 'One of these days, Kimberley Harris, you might really get to know me,' he said in a low tense voice. 'Let's hope, by then, it's not too late.'

He stood up. 'Are you going to give me that lift or not?'

Kim was shaking. She had wanted him to confront her, to shake her, kiss her, do anything but issue her with some kind of confusing ultimatum.

'Since we're both going from the same house, I don't suppose I can refuse,' she said woodenly.

'Thanks.' He grimaced in satisfaction. 'I'll be ready at seven-thirty.'

Kim spent an hour soaking in the bath. If Lawrence Cory wanted one, he would have to wait, she told herself nastily, but he didn't put in an appearance and she supposed he must have used the shower in the summer-house.

Why hadn't he done that all along and saved her the aggravation of his presence these past few days? At least then her pride might have remained intact. Because that was what was hurting her now, a painful, hollow ache deep inside that she felt powerless to assuage. But pride could heal more quickly than a heart.

It would be ridiculous, she told herself, to allow anything as foolish as the incident in the summer-house to haunt her. It pleased her to call it an 'incident'. It trivialised the whole thing. . .put it into some kind of acceptable perspective.

After all, it had obviously been trivial to him. A means of proving a couple of points, one of which being how irresistible he was, the other being that even she, ice-cold Virgo, had been unable to resist that fatal Gemini charm.

The painful part was that it was true. In his arms, 'ice-woman' had simply melted away. She cringed inside every time she remembered how easy a conquest she had been, but, for once, humiliation had brought a more positive side-effect. She now knew there was at least one man in the world whose embrace didn't turn her ice-cold with revulsion. The pity of it was that it had taken a man like Lawrence Cory to remove the scales from her eyes.

When she got out of the bath, she engrossed herself once more in the problem of attire. In the end, she chose a mid-length emerald-green silk dress, high at the front, but dipping to an almost daring V at the back. It clung smoothly, outlining, but not blatantly revealing, her curves. A cluster of tiny diamonds with a central emerald hung in each ear to complement the outfit.

The colour turned her blue eyes to turquoise and brought out the bronze lights in her thick brown hair, which she brushed until it gleamed.

Lawrence was in the living-room as Kim came downstairs, and as she entered his eyes swept over her in candid appraisal.

'*Enchanteresse*,' he murmured, with a gleam in his amber eyes that Kim thought was probably mockery.

She coloured, as his gaze lingered on her face, and half wished she hadn't made such an obvious effort to look her best. With his kind of conceit, he probably thought it was for his benefit, she thought with wry annoyance.

'Thanks,' she said stiffly, and forbore to comment on his appearance.

Dressed in a light suit with a matching silk shirt a shade or two darker, he looked handsomer than ever. Estelle had been right, Kim mused—his tan certainly added to his attractiveness, though wild horses wouldn't have dragged that admission from her.

She drove Lawrence to Estelle's house, finding it impossible to even begin a conversation, and wishing she'd had the strength of mind to suggest he take a taxi. He would probably have argued there was no such thing in the village and he would probably be right. The annoying part of it was that she would have to drive him back as well, unless, of course, he managed to make other arrangements.

With a bit of luck, he would attach himself to Simone, or some other hapless female, and she would be able to leave him to it and slip away early.

Thankfully, the journey was fairly short. Kim didn't

think she could have endured the tense silence of the drive had it been more prolonged.

Estelle was in the hallway when they arrived, looking very elegant in a full-length silver gown and making Kim glad she'd made the effort to dress up to the occasion.

'Kimberley! You look beautiful,' she cried, kissing Kim on both cheeks.

'And Lawrence. . .so handsome.' She kissed him. 'Welcome to you both!'

Kim murmured something appropriate, and smiled to hide her perturbation.

Simone was standing in the doorway of the main room, staring at Kim, her green eyes spitting fire.

She stood aside reluctantly as Estelle led the way into the drawing-room, contenting herself merely with a darting look of venom in answer to Kim's tentative smile. But she pushed her hand forcefully through Lawrence's arm as he drew level, pulling him to her side.

'Lawrence,' she said sweetly, 'I have been waiting for you.'

Estelle smiled over her shoulder as Simone dragged Lawrence off and Kim wondered if the move had been planned between them.

With Estelle's arm in hers, she was led into the nearest group.

The number of people assembled in the big drawing-room was much smaller than previously and, this time, the sexes were mixed.

The group to which Estelle was introducing Kim were all men, mainly young, and she was embarrassed to see frank admiration in more than one pair of dark eyes. It was a long time since she'd aroused so much male interest. The men she mixed with at home were mainly business acquaintances and, as managing director of her own firm, she'd encountered more deference than dalliance.

Estelle noted their interest too and laughed delightedly. 'We shall be dancing later,' she said gaily. 'So you will each have your chance to make closer acquaintance with our English friend.'

Kim smiled cynically to herself. It appeared that not only was Estelle matchmaking for Simone and Lawrence, but she seemed also to be doing her best to remove Kim from the running. Not that it mattered to her, but she wished she could tell Estelle that she was wasting her time, in her case, since Lawrence wasn't the smallest bit interested in Kim anyway.

Another guest claimed Estelle's attention.

'Excuse me for a moment, my dear,' she said. 'I will be back soon. If you should want a drink. . .'

She waved a hand in the direction of a trestle-table set up at one side of the room.

Kim nodded, but stayed put. She wasn't ready to drink yet and, in any case, she would have to watch her consumption if she was to be in any fit state to drive home. Lawrence, of course, would be under no such restriction, she thought with a touch of resentment.

Her eyes went automatically around the room, searching for a dark head which would stand out above the others. He was over by the french windows, leaning easily against the wall and smiling down into Simone's animated face.

A shaft of emotion pierced Kim's heart that seemed strangely like jealousy.

Sexual jealousy, of course, she derided herself. Given the circumstances, what else could it be? Going to bed with him didn't mean she owned him. . .not that she'd want to.

She would be damned if she would let herself fall prey to that kind of stupid, unnecessary punishment, she vowed, and began deliberately to circulate the room in search of a face she might recognise from among the female members of Estelle's family, but the room seemed full of strangers.

It was Paul Baron who eventually brought her a glass of champagne. Estelle had got swallowed up somewhere and Kim was on the edge of the crowd trying to carry on a conversation with a little dark woman, whose dialect was almost impossible to understand.

Paul smiled at the woman and drew Kim tactfully away. 'It is difficult for you, *non*?' he queried understandingly. He handed her the glass. 'Drink a little and relax.'

'Thanks,' she said gratefully. 'I'm afraid my French is a bit rusty.'

'But not as rusty as my English,' he said. 'Yet, we shall manage to converse a little.'

He was an attractive, kindly man, Kim noted appreciatively, and when he smiled he looked very much like Georges. Estelle and Paul had been lucky in love; and Pamela, in love with their son, looked set to be the same. But then, Lawrence Cory would say they had made their own luck.

Paul stayed and chatted to her about wines and Kim was surprised at how much interest there was to be found in the subject.

Music began to play and people began to dance. Almost before she knew it, Kim was swept into the centre of the room, which had been cleared of carpet. Her partner was one of the young men Estelle had first introduced to her and he was wearing a pleased smile as he took her into his arms to dance. And when the dance was finished, another eager partner took his place.

Kim wondered if they had tossed a coin to decide the order in which they should claim her, as she passed, a little dizzily, from one to the other.

Estelle's comment about dancing with her seemed to have been taken in the nature of an order, rather than an invitation, Kim thought in tired amusement, as they seemed to have embarked on a second round.

'If you don't mind,' she said to her latest partner, 'I think I need a little rest.'

As she turned from him, she walked straight into Lawrence Cory's arms.

'I was just about to sit down,' she told him a little stiffly. 'I'm sure you really don't want to dance.'

'Oh, but I do.'

His arms closed about her and he began to move on to the floor, leading her unwilling feet with easy rhythm.

Reluctantly she relaxed and, for the first time that evening, actually began to enjoy the movement.

'You really can dance,' she said in surprise.

'Thanks. You're not so bad yourself.' His lip curled in a wry smile. 'I wish it was always this easy to get you to follow my lead.'

Kim flashed him a brief, ironic smile. 'I'm sure you do.'

He made no attempt to hold her intimately or place his cheek against her hair, as some others were doing to the slow beat of the music.

Kim told herself she was glad he was keeping his distance, yet the brush of his body against hers was an almost unbearable excitement and she grew warm as her blood began to race.

To her consternation, she found she had to restrain herself from moving closer. . .from tightening her arm about his neck to draw his head to hers. . .

Damn the man, she swore silently. What magic did he use to creep behind her defences? She barely even liked him, and yet his touch was electric.

'What happened to Simone?' she asked coolly, to break the spell.

He shrugged. 'Nothing that I know of. Should something have happened?'

Kim bit her lip, wishing she hadn't started this. He was using her own spite as a stick to beat her with.

His mocking look goaded her, but she refused to be tempted into further indiscretion.

She shrugged irritably. It was suddenly impossible to go on being held in his arms in this detached way. She'd been taught to want more.

'Do you mind if we stop? I find it rather hot in here.'

He pulled back to look down into her flushed face. 'You do look a little warm,' he said. 'Perhaps we should go outside for some fresh air.'

'That wasn't an invitation to you to come with me. I'd prefer to be alone.'

'Same old song, Kim?' he said indifferently. 'Maybe it's time you changed the record.'

'Thanks, but. . .'

She didn't complete the sentence.

'Don't bother arguing,' he said. 'Let's go.' His hand grasped her arm roughly and he all but marched her across the room.

Kim gritted her teeth, trying to smile at the curious faces turned towards them as he cleared a path with his shoulder towards the tall windows.

It was a warm, clear evening, with streaks of flame

and yellow on the horizon heralding another beautiful day to follow.

Surrounded by beauty, as he led her deep into the lovely garden, Kim saw none of it.

Close to inexplicable tears, she jerked suddenly to a halt.

'This is as far as I go,' she told him fiercely.

'It's far enough.'

Roughly he pulled her into his arms, kissing her with a ruthless force that had her breathless. Taken by surprise, she had no time to erect the barriers. She felt her lips parting under his onslaught and was powerless to prevent the rise of a terrible yearning. She wanted this, his closeness, his warmth, the ardent touch of his hands on her. He had shown her a need as potent as any drug and was now bent on turning her into an addict, and here she was, going along with him every step of the way.

And when she left for home. . .what then?

There was no future in this and he knew it. It was just another manifestation of his mammoth ego, making sure she never forgot him, and she knew some part of her never would. The awful thing was to find that, for now, she didn't care. She was in his arms and it was easy to delude herself that she belonged there.

When at last he broke away, Kim stared at him dazedly, aware that her heart was still beating madly with unfulfilled excitement.

His face was flushed, his eyes steely bright and, to her astonishment, she saw that he was angry.

'That disposes of the doubt,' he said with a kind of grim satisfaction. 'Now perhaps we can talk. . .honest talk.'

She faced him uncertainly. 'I haven't a clue what you're talking about.'

'Haven't you?' His mouth was a tight, grim line and his hands bit cruelly into the softness of her upper arms.

'You're put me through an agony of remorse these past few days, Kimberley Harris. I rushed things in the summer-house, I know that, but I won't go on suffering for that mistake.'

His eyes burned into hers with almost mesmeric intensity. 'You were more than ready for me this time, so don't bother to deny it.'

'All right, I won't,' she bit back, her temper flaring to meet his. 'Now you've got what you want, may I go?'

His eyes narrowed to an icy glare.

'I haven't got what I want,' he said through clenched teeth. 'But I will.'

'Good!' Kim cried defiantly. 'And I hope you enjoy it.'

'Oh, I will!' he promised silkily. 'The next time I hold you in my arms. . .make love to you. . .it will be because you've asked me.' A thin smile curved his lips. 'Only make it soon, or I might get tired of waiting.'

Kim's breath hissed inwards.

'Don't hold your breath while you're waiting,' she grated. 'Because you'll suffocate before I'd ever ask *you* for *anything*.'

He dipped his head to kiss her lips briefly. When he looked up he was smiling. . .a grimly disturbing smile.

'I hope you never take up gambling,' he said, before he walked away. 'Because you'd lose your shirt.'

Lawrence Cory was up on the musicians' dais with Estelle, Paul and Simone when Kim eventually went back into the house. She was just in time to catch the birthday presentation. Somebody pressed a glass of champagne into her hand as she stood at the back of the room.

'. . .the deeds to Mill Cottage,' Paul was saying, as he handed a scroll of papers tied up with blue ribbon into Lawrence's hand. 'May you be happy there and raise many healthy children.'

A burst of laughter and applause greeted this and Kim thought she saw a faint tinge of colour in Lawrence's lean cheeks as he answered, 'Let's not put the horse before the cart.'

So, that had been the birthday surprise Estelle had been so mysterious about. She and Paul had given him Mill Cottage. This way, Estelle could be sure her 'second son' lived near at hand, Kim thought, aware of an awful sinking sensation. Was it also her way of ensuring he was more easily available to Simone?

The applause subsided and, almost in confirmation of Kim's niggling suspicion, Estelle cut in laughingly, 'Don't rush things, Paul. Firstly, he must find a wife.' She waved a hand around the room, sweeping it back towards the dais to where Simone stood beside her. 'Do you have anyone in mind yet?'

Lawrence's gaze circled the room, until his eyes met Kim's with what seemed like a question. If he was asking her subtly for her opinion of Simone as his wife, then he would be disappointed. She had no comment to make.

A frown of annoyance showed momentarily in his face, as he probed her closed expression, but he was smiling as he turned his attention back to the people beside him on the dais.

'I'm working on it,' he said.

Another burst of laughter arose, and Simone threw herself into his arms, smothering him with rapturous kisses. Kim saw his hands go around her slim waist, holding her to him.

There was a sick, hollow feeling in the pit of Kim's stomach.

Minutes ago, he'd been holding her in his arms, kissing her with a passion that couldn't be faked. He'd awakened in her a hopeless kind of hope; a tiny glimmer of what could be, if only. . .

Everyone seemed bent on congratulating Lawrence Cory. They shook his hands, it being impossible to kiss him because Simone was there, clinging around his neck, practically delirious with delight.

Kim laughed, a soft ironic sound.

The net was closing around Lawrence Cory and he deserved everything that was coming to him. She ought to be glad, she told herself disgustedly, but knew she couldn't stay to be in at the kill.

If she left now, it would have to be without taking her leave of Estelle or Paul, but she would make her apologies tomorrow, plead a headache if necessary. . .which wouldn't be too far from the truth, the way she felt at the moment.

And Lawrence Cory would have to make his own way back; that was if he didn't decide to stay the night at Estelle's, once he discovered Kim had gone on home without him.

A light was on in the hallway and living-room of the cottage she noted as she parked her car in the small driveway. For a moment she felt nervous. After the uproar of the party, the rest of the world seemed a very silent empty place.

But whoever it was in the cottage, she reasoned, would hardly advertise their presence with a blaze of lights if they intended anything sinister.

None the less, she inserted her key in the front door as silently as she could manage and turned it slowly. She jumped back in shock as the door opened forcefully from within.

'Kim! At last! I was beginning to wonder if you were ever coming home.'

'Charles!' she gasped faintly. 'What on earth are you doing here?'

'I came to see you, of course.' His laugh sounded a little forced. 'I thought you might be pleased to see me.'

'Of course I'm pleased to see you.' She kissed his cheek. 'It's such a complete surprise, that's all. How did you get from the airport this late at night?'

'I didn't. I motored down here. I arrived nearly three hours ago.'

'What?' Kim stared at him in astonishment. 'But why didn't you let me know you were coming? I've been expecting you to ring all week.'

'I wanted to surprise you.' He took her arm and began to lead her into the living-room. 'Let's have a cup of tea and talk about it.'

Talk about what? Kim wondered, with a sinking sensation, but there was no point in deluding herself, of course. Charles was here to pursue his proposal and it was a measure of his determination that he'd taken time off from his precious business to drive all the way down to the cottage to persuade her. She only hoped her determination was equal to his.

'You go on through and sit down,' she said, hearing the shake in her voice. Her nerves must be more ragged than she thought. 'I'll make the tea and fetch it in.'

He was pacing the room when she carried the tray in, something else she had never seen him do. He was obviously tense and wound-up. Without giving her a chance even to pour the tea, he sat down beside her and took her hands in his.

'I know you said we would talk when you got back home, but I couldn't wait. I haven't had a minute's peace since that phone call the other night.'

He cleared his throat and seemed to be having difficulty going on, but at last he said, 'I may have bungled things last time we were alone together, Kim, but you know how I feel about you and I suppose I just got carried away. That's why I thought it would be better if I came and stayed a while; to ask you again and give you time to think calmly.'

'Charles,' Kim began, and paused to take a deep breath. 'I have been thinking quite a bit, and I really don't believe there's any point in all this.'

There was no avoiding the issue now. Even without Lawrence's intervention in her life, she knew, without the smallest doubt, that marriage to Charles would have been the biggest mistake of her life. As much for his sake as for hers, she had to make him see it was impossible.

'I'm sorry, but. . . I don't want to marry you. . . I. . .can't.'

She stopped, shocked by the look on his suddenly pale face. He seemed to stop breathing for a long moment and then the blood rushed up his neck and into his cheeks, a peculiar plum shade which had Kim worrying about his blood-pressure.

'You don't mean it,' he gasped. 'We've always known we would marry. It was just a matter of when.'

His hands grasped her arms, and he stared at her with pink-tinged, disbelieving eyes. 'I can't believe you've changed your mind.'

She shook her head, dismayed by his distress, but

knowing she was right and mustn't weaken. 'I haven't changed my mind, Charles. It was never made up. And now I know I may never marry, unless. . .'

She'd been about to say unless she met another man who, like Lawrence Cory, could burn away her resistance with a kiss of fire.

He stared at her, a deep frown on his fair brow. 'It's him, isn't it? This Cory bloke. He's swept you off your feet.'

'Don't be ridiculous,' Kim protested. 'It has nothing to do with him.'

But he wasn't listening to her.

'This damned wedding has put stars in your eyes. You'd be easy prey for a smoothie like him.'

Kim flushed with a mixture of anger and humiliation. She might harbour such suspicions herself about Lawrence, but she didn't want Charles dragging out into the open all her hidden doubts.

'Thanks for the vote of confidence. I'm hardly that naïve.'

Charles stood up suddenly, dragging her up into his arms. 'I love you, Kim,' he said jerkily. 'And I know you love me.'

'No, I don't. You're wrong.' She was startled by his unexpected desperation. 'I don't love anyone. I don't even believe I know what love is——'

'Bravo!'

Kim was startled by the voice and the sound of hands clapping together.

'A little insight, at last, *Miss Harris*.' Lawrence's cynical voice cut through the charged atmosphere. 'And I agree with you, but only up to a point.'

He was standing in the doorway, lounging insolently and clapping his hands with a slow, sharp sound.

'What are you doing here?' She glared at him, all the

irritations of the evening coming to a head as she saw his mocking smile. She shrugged Charles's hands from her arms and went towards him, her face a mask of fury.

'Have I been giving out radar signals again, *Mr Cory*?' she spat. 'I'm convinced that's how you always manage to turn up at the most inconvenient times.'

'I know! Uncanny, isn't it? We seem drawn to each other by some irresistible force, don't we?'

'Answer my question,' she commanded. 'Why are you here?'

'You walked out on me,' he said casually. 'So I came to find you.'

'Kim! Have you really been going out with this fellow?'

Charles's hard-edged query went unnoticed as Kim lost herself in the familiar battle with Lawrence Cory.

'I don't know why you should bother,' she bit back, her eyes chips of blue ice.

He laughed. 'Neither do I. But I'm glad I arrived just in time to catch your unexpected words of wisdom. But you're wrong on one count.'

'You're probably dying to tell me which one,' Kim said bitterly. 'But I'm just not interested in hearing it.'

His brows rose. 'Not even the tiniest bit curious?'

'Kim. I insist you tell me. . .what's been going on?'

'Not a lot,' Lawrence said, his eyes still on Kim's face. 'But I'm hoping the situation will improve.'

'Well, you'll be a long time hoping,' Kim retorted.

Charles moved forward and gripped Kim's arm, pushing her forcefully away from Lawrence. He eyed him aggressively.

'I'm trying to have a private conversation with my fiancée, Cory.'

Kim stared at him, shocked into silence by this

unexpected and grossly inaccurate declaration, but she quickly recovered.

'That's right,' she said, to add weight to Charles's assertion. 'So, perhaps you'd be kind enough to leave.'

The amusement died out of Lawrence Cory's face. 'I'm not feeling particularly kind tonight.'

He came and stood before her, ignoring Charles, who seemed about to burst with anger. 'As the new owner of Mill Cottage, I've decided to take up residence as of now. So, if you'll excuse me, I'll be off to bed. Goodnight.'

'But you can't.' Kim stepped to bar his way as he made for the hallway and the stairs. 'There are only two bedrooms.'

'That's right.' He nodded. 'You're welcome to remain, of course. What sleeping arrangements you make for your fiancé. . .' he paused at the word to give it derisive emphasis '. . .are your affair, but I have to say that I don't approve of promiscuity under my roof.'

Speechless for the second time in a matter of seconds, Kim glared at him, infuriated all the more by the raised brow and the cynical twist of his mouth. Him! Of all people! To talk about promiscuity.

'But it's all right in the summer-house, I suppose,' she said, goaded beyond discretion. 'Why, you. . .hypocritical. . .!'

She flew at him, bent on smacking the smug expression from his face, but Charles was there before her, standing in her way.

'I want an explanation of that remark, Cory.'

'And I might give you one, if it were any of your business.' Lawrence's bright amber eyes narrowed on Charles's pale grey ones. 'My advice is to ask Kim to repeat what she has just said to you. . .only this time, you should listen.'

'When I want your advice, Cory, I'll ask for it.'

Charles's face was stained bright red with anger, and Kim saw his fists bunching aggressively. 'If there weren't a lady present I'd give you a good hiding.'

Lawrence laughed easily. 'I doubt it. But if you're still of the same mind in the morning I might give you the opportunity to try.'

'Don't think I won't take you up on that,' Charles growled.

'I'd be delighted if you did,' Lawrence said cynically. 'Except that I suspect Kim would hand herself as a consolation prize to the loser, and that would be disastrous.'

He moved past them both towards the hall.

'Now, if you'll excuse me, I'll say goodnight.'

Kim was up early and getting breakfast in the kitchen when Charles put in an appearance.

They'd had a heated discussion, after Lawrence had gone to bed, about who should sleep upstairs. Lawrence had taken over the main room with its twin beds. Had the situation been different, Charles might have shared with him, but that was obviously now impossible. There was only a single in Kim's room, but she could hardly have shared a room with Charles anyway.

'I'm sleeping in my own room,' she'd insisted hotly. 'There's a lock on it and I'm damned if Lawrence Cory is going to turf me out of my own bed.'

'I won't have you alone up there with him, Kimberley,' Charles had insisted, with a stubborn look Kim had never seen before. 'I would never be able to sleep a wink for worrying.'

'Well, that's your problem.' Kim's temper had been

dangerously frayed. 'You can sleep on the couch or take yourself off to the summer-house. Either way, it's up to you, but I'm off to bed.'

He'd slept, fully dressed, on the sofa in the end. Kim had tiptoed past him on her way to the kitchen. She'd been quiet, but the movement must have disturbed him.

'Good morning, Charles,' she greeted him, as he came into the kitchen. 'I hope you haven't bothered to unpack, because I'll be ready to leave shortly.'

She looked at the clock, which said eight-thirty. She'd been up since before six, pushing all her belongings into her cases. Her clothes would all need laundering when she got home, to rid them of the creases, but that was a minor consideration when faced with her need to get away quickly.

With Lawrence's taking over possession of the house and Charles in his present mood, the last few days of her intended stay would be more like hell than a holiday. It was time to retire gracefully.

'Ready to leave?' He echoed. 'I thought you were staying for the rest of the week. I didn't drive all the way down here to rush back again the following day.'

'I know. And I'm sorry. But if you'd telephoned me to say you were coming I'd have told you not to bother.'

'I'm sure you would have and that's precisely why I didn't telephone.' Charles was still truculent, Kim noted with a sigh. 'After my last call, I just had to find out what's been happening here with Cory.'

Kim glared at him indignantly. 'What I do with Cory, or with anyone else for that matter, is my business,' she said, her temper dangerously frayed. 'Despite what you implied to Lawrence Cory last night, I am not your fiancée and I do *not* owe you any explanations.'

He reached for her hand, but she snatched it away.

He sighed. 'I've jumped the gun a little, I know,' he began apologetically. 'But when you get back home and come down to earth again, you'll forget all this nonsense, and we can carry on from where we left off.'

'Down to earth', Kim thought with a shudder. He couldn't have chosen a more chilling description. These past ten days she'd taken flight. She remembered the lines of the song she'd heard, about taking a trip to the moon on gossamer wings. A fantasy. But she knew she would never quite come down to earth again. There would always be the magic to remember. To carry on with Charles where she'd left off would be impossible, but there was no point in trying to persuade him of that now.

'I'm leaving as soon as I've finished packing,' she said purposefully. 'I want to get off early, before the traffic builds up.'

Charles regarded her with eyes that were suddenly shrewd.

'Or before Cory comes down,' he said thickly. '*If* he comes down. My guess is he'll stay well away,' he added derisively. 'If he knows what's good for him, he will.'

Kim gave a short laugh. 'Don't be ridiculous, Charles. Despite what Lawrence Cory said last night, I will definitely not be awarding myself as prize to the loser of any stupid fight. Neither do I intend to hang about here ready to give you first aid.'

'Thanks! I'm beginning to get the message.' His face reddened. 'You fancy yourself in love with the fellow, don't you?' There was a jeering note in his voice and Kim opened her mouth to give a fiery retort.

She closed it again as his accusation sank in.

I don't fancy myself in love with him, she thought,

with a sick, sinking feeling. I really am in love with him, and there isn't a thing I can do about it.

Now she was leaving there was no point in denying it, not even to herself.

But she would never, never admit it to Lawrence Cory.

His future had been neatly sewn up by Estelle and Simone, with a little willing help from Lawrence himself, so all that remained to be done now was to wish them all well of it.

'I'm leaving in half an hour,' she said, deadly calm. 'If you're coming you'd better be ready.'

Charles snorted derisively.

'You don't imagine I'm going to run away from Cory, do you? I should think you'd know me better than that.'

I've suddenly realised I don't know you at all, Kim told herself silently, surprised to find that made her feel more relieved than sad.

'Then stay and fight it out, if that's what you want.'

She didn't add that there was nothing left worth fighting for.

CHAPTER TEN

KIM was packing her luggage into the boot of her car as a sleek sporty car drew up outside the cottage and Simone got out, closely followed by a young man in overalls.

'Where's Lawrence?' she demanded, without preamble.

'Still in bed,' Kim answered coolly. 'But if I were you I wouldn't go barging in there just at the moment.'

Lawrence would hardly be pleased to have Simone discover him involved in a fight with another man caused, however indirectly, by another woman.

'But you aren't me, are you, *chérie*?' Simone said, with arch mockery. 'Though I suspect you wish you were.'

Kim coloured faintly, annoyed to realise how close to the truth that was.

Why was she even bothering to argue anyway? Whatever happened now, it was none of her business.

'You're welcome to wait for Lawrence in the kitchen,' she replied calmly. 'He should be getting up shortly. Make yourself a cup of coffee.'

'I don't want your coffee,' Simone sneered. 'And I certainly don't want your advice.' Her eyes narrowed suspiciously. 'But why is Lawrence sleeping in the house? I thought he was staying in the summer-house.'

'It was his decision to sleep where he did,' she said with a gleeful malice. 'I think you should ask him to explain his reasons.'

That should put a few cats among the pigeons.

Simone's green eyes glared at her malevolently. 'Whatever the explanation, *chérie*, it appears you have lost.'

'Looks like it,' Kim admitted, with a shrug. 'I wish you better luck.'

'I won't need it.' She gave a triumphant smile and turned away.

'Luc!' she called commandingly to the young man in overalls. 'Go and check in the shed to see if the tools you need are there.'

He nodded and went off down the garden.

Kim frowned. 'What tools? What is he going to do?'

'He has been sent here by my uncle to do the garden,' Simone answered shortly. 'Not that it is any of your business.' Her mouth curved tauntingly. 'Very soon, however, it will be my business.'

Kim refrained, with an effort, from retorting that the cottage was still under hire, paid for by Pamela. She was leaving now, so what did it matter?

So! It was all fixed up between Lawrence and the French girl, she thought ruefully. Simone hadn't wasted any time in calling around to gloat.

'Congratulations!' she managed rather tightly. 'I'm sure you'll suit one another very well.'

'So am I.' Simone's cat-like smile taunted Kim.

Maybe they really were two of a kind, Kim mused. Simone certainly had the same kind of grim determination as Lawrence, and perhaps he'd known all along what Estelle had planned for him, should he decide to buy the Daumier business and settle in France.

What Kim couldn't work out was why he should have bothered to dally with her in the first place. Perhaps it had been his last fling before settling down. Or maybe he had just been unable to resist the challenge of getting her into bed with him.

Whatever the reason, he had got her into bed, and willingly too, as he'd predicted. That accomplished, it appeared he was now ready to commit himself to marriage with Simone.

A pain began deep inside Kim. Why hadn't he left her alone—safe in her own unemotional world, never knowing what else that other world of the senses had to offer? What you never have you never miss. An old cliché, but painfully true in her case. Having lain in Lawrence's arms, she now knew only too well what she would always be missing.

Kim kept her mind deliberately on the road ahead as she got out of the village and on to the motorway. With an almost feverish desperation, she longed for the journey to be over. Her cramped little flat, a thirty-minute drive away from her office, seemed to beckon like a harbour of safety. All she wanted now was to arrive there, and to settle back into the predictable routine of work.

Perhaps Charles was right. Away from the cottage and Lawrence Cory, the uneasy memories would cease to haunt her. Maybe it would be possible to settle back into her comfortable rut and fill her days with the work she had always found so satisfying. There was still the best part of a day's drive to the hotel. But at least there would be no Lawrence Cory to irritate her with his presence and, with a bit of luck, she might manage a relaxing meal and a good night's sleep.

The booking she'd made with Monsieur Dubois for the return-journey stop-over was still some days away, but she hoped he would be able to bring it forward to let her have a room for tonight. The hotel hadn't been anywhere near full on the way down, so she didn't think she'd have too much trouble.

She looked at the dashboard clock, which said almost eleven, and wondered what had been the outcome of Charles's anticipated fight. With Simone on the premises, it was hardly likely Lawrence would allow himself a confrontation with the enraged 'fiancé' of another woman. Now Kim was gone, he would probably have lost interest in the game anyway.

She came out of her reverie as a car, travelling in the faster lane, suddenly pulled into the slow lane in front of her, causing her to brake to avoid hitting the back end.

'Fool!' she shouted aloud to vent her feelings.

It was bad enough trying to keep her car on the road as it was, without having to put up with some idiot who couldn't drive intelligently.

The man in the car in front was signalling something to her, pointing a little way ahead to a lay-by. Did he expect her to stop so that he could apologise? Hardly likely, she thought with a somewhat shaky laugh. He was probably some French Romeo who couldn't help showing off to any passing female.

Still, it was annoying; he kept slowing, forcing her to brake in order to keep her distance, but soon she was so close that she could see his face in the rear-view mirror.

Lawrence Cory, she realised with a sickening jolt. What on earth was he doing here driving a car alone? And whose car was it?

Suddenly, her mind clicked into gear.

It was Charles's car, she realised in astonishment, but there was no sign of Charles himself. What on earth had happened?

Lawrence was slowing almost to a crawl in front of her. He was signalling to pull into the lay-by and Kim had no option but to follow him. He was out of the car almost before hers had shuddered to a stop.

'Kim!' He pulled open her door and dragged her out into his arms. 'You didn't think I'd let you get away with it, did you?'

Get away with what? Kim wondered dazedly, as he enveloped her in a tight hug, which almost squeezed the breath from her body. Her heart began to race unsteadily with a glimmer of hope.

'What on earth are you doing here?' she asked, when at last she could speak. 'And in Charles's car—does he know you've got it?'

'I expect he does by now.' Lawrence smiled grimly. 'But let's get back to you. Is that the best I deserve? You running off without saying goodbye or giving me your address?'

'Why should you want my address? Were you hoping we'd become pen-pals?'

'You know what I was hoping,' he growled. 'It's just that damned stubborn pride of yours that won't let you admit you want the same thing.'

Kim felt a light-headed desire to laugh.

'You may consider yourself psychic,' she said bitingly, 'but in my case, you're way off the mark.'

Did he actually expect her to admit she loved him in return for his admission of lust? And to come chasing after her in this fashion! She would never have believed him capable of going to such lengths to make sure he didn't lose a conquest.

He shook her fiercely. 'If you think I'm going to go through the same old arguments with you here on a frantic French motorway, you're mad.'

'It is a bit public,' she observed coolly.

He scowled at her attempted levity. 'I can do without the jokes. We need to sort things out and, with your belligerent fiancé waiting at the cottage, we're not going to have much peace to talk back there.'

'I don't think there's anything to talk about,' Kim said a little shakily. 'And, talking of *fiancées*, I don't imagine Simone will take kindly to your chasing up the motorway after another woman. It's not the kind of behaviour a woman expects from the man she is to marry.'

His brows lifted. 'Simone told you we're going to be married?'

'As good as,' Kim said with a cynical laugh. 'Why? Is it a secret?'

He made a short, impatient sound. 'Only from me.'

Without giving her a chance to ask what he meant by that, he grasped Kim's arm and bundled her into the car.

'I'm coming on with you to the hotel. You take this car and I'll take your boyfriend's.'

'But what about Charles?' Kim protested. 'He'll be wanting his car. He's supposed to be coming on home later today.'

'Tough!' Lawrence gave a hard laugh. 'He'll just have to wait at the cottage until I get back. Simone and he can comfort one another. Who knows? With a bit of luck they might hit it off together and save us both a lot of trouble.'

He banged his hand against the roof of the car. 'Drive on to the hotel,' he commanded. 'I'll be right behind you.'

Lawrence drew up behind her in the car park at the back of the hotel and jumped out. She'd been sitting there for four or five minutes waiting for him, wondering what was in that devilish mind of his now. For a little while she'd been free of him and all the turmoil he created.

Why had she even agreed to come here with him? She should have sent him back with Charles's car and come on alone. But with Lawrence, of course, there was no guaranteeing his co-operation in any of her plans.

'How did you manage to pull so far ahead?' he queried a little irritably. 'I thought I'd lost you.'

'I don't know.' Kim shrugged. 'I wasn't driving that fast.'

She looked him over and felt a silly urge to laugh.

He'd quite obviously rushed into his clothes, because his cream trousers were creased and his short-sleeved shirt was done up on a wrong button. His hair stood on end as though it hadn't seen a comb in a month, and his chin was showing an urgent need for a razor.

'Jump out!' he said imperiously. 'I'll get your luggage.'

'Don't bring it all,' Kim said. 'One case will do. You can leave the rest where it is.'

'OK. So long as you don't mind playing lucky dip on what's available to wear.'

'I won't be worrying about that,' she said firmly, and then laughed. 'I don't think anyone's going to be noticing me anyway, the way you look.'

She undid the buttons of his shirt and did them all up again in the proper order.

She saw the quickening of his breath as her fingers brushed against the dark springy hairs of his chest.

His eyes, as she gazed up at him in surprise, were alight with something that spelled danger, and she knew she'd been a fool to go anywhere near him. Hastily, she handed him a comb.

'Do something with your hair. You look positively wild.'

'That's about how I feel.' He dragged the comb quickly through his hair, grimacing at the tangles.

'I'm going inside to see if I can get a room for the night,' she said pointedly. 'You'll be lucky to be let in at all, when they see the state you're in. Still, I don't suppose it matters for the hour or so you'll be staying.'

'You don't imagine I'll be rushing back to the cottage, do you? I'm stopping the night.'

Looking into his grimly determined face, Kim knew there was no point in arguing with him.

It was strange to be walking into the hotel again together. It seemed a lifetime ago that he'd followed her up these same steps, carrying her baggage. They'd been strangers then. And it had been his birthday, she thought inconsequentially.

What was it her birthday horoscope had said about a 'stranger's act of kindness' leading to romance? Well, in a way, it had, although romance wasn't quite the word she would have chosen to describe what had happened between them. And his horoscope had promised success in business and a stormy love-match. Simone was certainly that, she thought with a surge of resentment.

She studied the strong contours of his face, as he dropped her case to the floor and punched the big brass bell on the reception desk, hiding a smile of grudging approval. He was a man who would always be capable of looking after himself.

Disconcertingly, he caught her gaze.

'This is quite like old times, isn't it?' He grinned at her, and an answering smile tugged at the corners of her mouth.

'Times I'd rather forget,' she said quellingly.

'Really?' He raised his brows.

'Really!' she said, and hit the bell hard.

The last time they were here, he'd claimed her as his wife and told everyone they were on honeymoon. A wild flight of fantasy that had no chance of ever becoming reality.

Monsieur Dubois seemed pleased to see them, treating them like long-lost friends and seeming not to notice anything wrong with Lawrence's appearance.

'I have rooms on the same floor this time, if you wish.' He beamed.

'Yes, thanks,' Lawrence said, at the same time as Kim said,

'That won't be necessary, thank you.'

She glared at Lawrence's mocking face as she added, 'I require a single room, *not* interconnecting with his.'

'Coward,' Lawrence said softly.

His nearness and the warmth of his breath close to her ear had Kim's toes curling. It just wasn't safe to be around him, and she'd be glad when tomorrow came and he would be gone.

'What time is dinner?' he asked, as he signed the register.

'Eight o'clock, *monsieur*.'

'Good!' Lawrence nodded. 'That will give me time to have a bath.' He rubbed at his chin and even that gesture had Kim's spine chilling. 'I need a shave. You haven't got a razor I could use, have you?'

'But of course.'

From beneath the desk-top, Monsieur Dubois produced a packet of disposable razors, with the air of a magician pulling a rabbit from a hat.

'*Voilà!*'

'I think I'd stick with the designer stubble,' Kim

advised drily. 'Just in case you meet any more of your fans. I won't be bailing you out this time.'

Kim came down to dinner wearing a soft yellow cotton dress with front scoop neckline and a low back. The colour complemented her honey-tanned skin and glowing blue eyes.

He, of course, was still in the casual shirt and cream trousers, but his hair was clean and gleaming with vitality. He hadn't shaved after all and the already thickening stubble added to rather than detracted from his good looks.

He met her in the small lounge and escorted her immediately to the dining-room. It was little more than half full, and this time there was no one who seemed remotely interested in Lawrence Cory as a celebrity.

Kim sighed with relief. She felt almost light-hearted as the waiter directed them to a table for two close to the window which looked on to the garden.

'Let's eat first and talk after,' Lawrence said as they settled at their table. 'I'm starving.'

Kim nodded her approval of that suggestion. She was also suddenly very hungry.

'I don't really see what good talking will do,' she said, as they finished their meal and the waiter served coffee.

'How else are we going to communicate?' he asked sardonically.

'You know what I mean,' she said irritably. 'I don't even know what you're doing here. Haven't you got enough? Estelle dotes on you and can't wait for you to take up residence in her wonderful birthday present, Mill Cottage.'

'Interesting!' he said, softly goading. 'But do go on.'

She knew he was loving this, but felt too incensed to stop.

'She's even thrown Simone in as further bait to make sure you don't lack anything to keep you happy in France.' She gave a cynical little laugh. 'I think, if I were in your place, I'd look on that particular young lady more as a fly in the ointment than an inducement, but there's no accounting for taste.'

His mouth curved slowly upwards, his eyes darkening as he fixed her with an intent look. 'You're jealous of Simone!'

Kim's face flamed. She'd given herself away, and he obviously wasn't going to spare her the revelation.

'Don't be ridiculous. Why should I care if you're taken in by that pretty, feline face? Simone's your problem.'

He gave a short laugh. 'Not if I can help it, she isn't.'

She gave him a guarded look. 'You mean the wedding's off?'

'No. That is not what I mean,' he said with exaggerated patience. 'What I mean is there was never going to be a wedding in the first place.'

Kim hid a smile of malicious satisfaction. 'Simone's going to be disappointed. It's a pity you didn't make it clear to her how you felt about marriage.'

He grunted in disgust. 'How do you get Simone to hear anything when she doesn't want to listen?'

'You tell me.' Kim shrugged. 'But Estelle had plans in the same direction too. You and Simone together under her maternal wing.'

'That might have been her idea at first,' he said enigmatically. 'But I think you may discover that she's changed course a little, since then, on the subject of my marriage.'

He was staring into the dregs of his coffee, engrossed

in the vision he could see there. 'Marriage was the last thing on my mind when I came out here. All I wanted was to do a little business and have a peaceful time lazing about.'

That and a little idle seduction, Kim thought bitterly.

'What went wrong?' she asked with an attempt at lightness.

'You,' he said abruptly, and stood up.

Startled, she stared up at him, trying to see his meaning in his face, but his taut expression gave nothing away.

'Your place or mine?' He tugged at her arm to make her rise. 'This dining-room is a little public.'

'For what?' She eyed him suspiciously, her pulses already racing. 'If you think you can get away with a repetition of——'

'My room has a nice private little balcony. Let's go.' He pulled her to her feet.

She was tempted to struggle, but it seemed so undignified and people were beginning to take an interest.

'All right,' she capitulated, 'but no funny business.'

'I assure you I'm deadly serious.'

'Not that deadly, I hope,' she said in a sorry attempt at humour. She had that strange, overwhelming feeling of inevitability as she allowed him to lead her to the door of his room.

'I'm not sure I should be doing this,' she said in sudden doubt, as he fished in his pocket for his key.

'Don't worry.' His grin had a mocking twist to it. 'If Charlie-boy wants to know what happened beyond this door, tell him to ask me. I'll put him right.'

'The way you tried to do at the cottage, tricking me almost into giving myself away.'

He forgot about the key and gripped her shoulders

with sudden fierceness. 'You didn't give yourself *away*. You gave yourself to *me*.'

'A moment of madness I'll always regret,' she said, watching an angry spark grow in his flame-coloured eyes. 'None of which concerns Charles, by the way. I'm my own person.'

The frown on his brow dispersed. 'You mean you've broken off your engagement?'

'Like you, I was never engaged,' she said, with a grim little smile.

Lawrence's eyes turned bright and glittering. 'You mean you were never getting married either?'

'Not quite true,' she had to admit. 'I might have married Charles eventually if. . .' She paused. She'd been about to say if you hadn't shown me the error of my ways, but went on instead, 'If things had turned out differently.'

His expression was disconcertingly intent, his eyes searching for secrets in her own. With an effort, she tore her gaze away.

'After my painful experience of men,' she rushed on, 'I think I'll opt for Pamela's predicted life of lonely Virgo virginity.'

As soon as she saw his face, she knew she'd made a mistake.

'Or, if you wish to split hairs,' she added a little stridently, 'near-virginity.'

He put his hand against her mouth in mock anxiety. 'Hush. Do you want the whole hotel to hear you?'

Kim freed herself with an irritable shake of her head. 'Actually, I'm past caring.' She glared at him. 'Somewhere along the line, I seem to have developed a skin almost as thick as yours.'

He fished his key out of his pocket at last, and opened the door.

'Oh! I have my weak spots.' He smiled comspiratorially and took her elbow. 'Come inside and let me show you a few.'

The suggestion seemed full of the most terrifying possibilities.

'Thanks. But no thanks.'

'It's not an invitation.' His grip tightened and he pushed the door wide, ushering her in before him. 'It's an order.'

It was a bigger place than her small single room—in fact, it was almost a suite. Some part of Kim's brain registered the fact with surprising clarity. It had a small vestibule before the main room, which had a lounge area as well as a bed.

She stopped in surprise, and took a couple of steps backwards.

'You've got a double bed!' she exclaimed accusingly.

He nodded, an amused curl to his lips. 'I like to spread myself out.'

'As well as around?' Kim suggested a little crudely.

He grinned and came and put his hands on her shoulders. 'I like the way your eyes glint icy blue when you're jealous.'

Kim opened her mouth to deny his accusation, but closed it again. What was the point?

'Besides, it's not that way any more.' He brushed a stray wisp of hair from her cheeks, his cool fingers spreading fire. 'Not since I met maddening, irritating, cool Miss Virgo. Nowadays I'm only willing to share fifty-fifty.' He pulled her closer. 'Here's my fifty per cent. . .where's yours. . .?'

She struggled and he let her push him away. She walked towards the balcony and opened the tall doors to go outside. Somehow she felt safer in the open air.

'If you were under orders from Pamela to make my

acquaintance on the trip over to France, why didn't you approach me on the ferry and introduce yourself properly?'

'I was under no instructions from Pamela; she simply mentioned you were coming out on the same crossing. I said I'd look out for you, but, frankly, I thought the whole thing would be a bit of a bore.'

He came and stood alongside her at the rail.

'Actually, her description of you was quite graphic and I thought probably overstated, but I had no difficulty picking you out from the rest.' His hand toyed with the hair at the nape of her neck. 'I'll admit once I actually saw you I was intrigued.'

She shrugged away from his touch and turned to face him. 'But not enough to introduce yourself.'

'You've described yourself as cold.' He thrust his hands into his pockets, as though to keep from touching her. 'I saw the coldness too, but thought it was probably fear.'

'Fear of what?' Kim felt as though he was stripping her bare, not physically, but deep inside, turning her inside-out, bringing dark things to the light, but she seemed unable to pretend any more. She wanted to know.

'Of the unknown, I suppose. Of what might be if you once let go of that iron control.'

She gave him a grim smile. 'And you were tempted to help me let go and find out?'

'Not at first. I felt it would take time to get you to drop that heavy guard, and time was something I wasn't willing then to devote to a strange lady who was obviously going to give me trouble. I had my own future to sort out and, even to please Pamela, I wasn't about to take on your problems.'

I didn't have any until you came along, she thought

ironically, but knew it wasn't true. She felt inside, searching for the cold hard lump which had lived in her for so long, but there was only the warm, pulsating beat of her heart.

'Then why did you bother?' She had to go on.

'I didn't. And perhaps I never would have if we hadn't met again at the motorway services.'

'Did you bump into me on purpose?' she asked with sudden suspicion.

'No. That was pure chance.' He shrugged. 'Fate stepping in. As soon as I heard your voice, saw the fire burning behind those lovely eyes, I began to believe it might be worth the trouble to get to know you. . .to get through that barrier and beyond.'

He took his hands from his pockets with a sudden, jerking movement, as though he couldn't bear the restraint another minute. He grasped her upper arms and drew her towards him.

'Am I getting through to you, Kimberley?'

She tried to back away from him. 'You said we were here to talk.'

'I'm talking,' he said softly. 'Can't you hear?'

She stared at him, aware of the tremor of excitement building up inside her. He was conning her again, she was sure, but she didn't want him to stop.

His eyes smiled mysteriously into her wide gaze.

'I'm telling you the truth, the whole truth and nothing but the truth. Let's see if you can work it out.'

His lips descended suddenly, giving her no chance to answer, the thrust of his tongue invading her mouth with sweet urgency, his hands warm and persuasive against the bare skin of her back, chafing against the restriction of her clothing.

This was madness and she knew it, but she wanted him to make love to her, her need clear and stark against the confusion of her mind. There was no past, no future, no right, no wrong. . .there was only this longing to taste again the sweet ecstacy of his loving.

She clung to him, exchanging kiss for burning kiss, until she thought she would burst into flames. She heard the sound of her own ragged breathing and his, like an echo, as his lips and hands urged her on to greater rapture.

He paused suddenly, lifting his head to look down into her flushed face. 'Do you want to go on?'

She nodded, letting her eyes, wide and dewy with excitement, tell him what he wanted to know.

He shook his head. 'You have to say it, Kim. So I'll know there's no mistake.'

He moved away a little and her hands clutched at him, drawing him back again.

Her lips parted, but no words came out. Once she spoke, he would always know she was his just for the taking. And what if. . .after her surrender. . .he never wanted her again? a frightened voice asked.

He wanted her now and that had to be enough.

'Yes or no?' he demanded insistently.

'Yes!' Kim said. 'Oh, yes!'

He growled, a sound of savage satisfaction, and put his lips again to hers.

In a rapturous daze, Kim felt the clothes slipping from her, and somehow he too was naked. She gasped at the sensation of his hard, aroused body against hers.

He bent again, his mouth caressing her arched throat, moving downwards to her eager breasts, tantalising her into a startling moan of raw need. He looked up exultantly and smiled as she arched herself against him.

Swiftly, he lifted her and carried her to the bed, where he put her gently down and lay beside her.

He kissed her, his hand moving against her feverish skin, moulding her hardened breasts, sweeping across the taut muscles of her stomach, his fingers seeking and finding the source of a sudden, fierce pleasure. A crescendo was building inside her, a fire which only he could quench.

She pulled at his shouders, telling him urgently, wordlessly of her desire, a joyous smile beginning as he moved to cover her body with his own.

Then, suddenly, he was wrenching away, sending painful waves of shock through her sensitised body.

'No, Kim!'

She stared at him, full of a terrible kind of emptiness. 'But I want you!' she cried. 'And you want me. I know you do.'

He shook his head. 'Not like this.'

'Then how?' she wailed. 'For pity's sake, Lawrence. Don't make me go on saying it. I want you to love me.'

She heard the sharp intake of his breath.

His hands gripped her face.

'For how long? Until I've thawed you out of your tower of ice. And then what?'

Kim's heart was beginning to sing.

The mirror image of her own fear. . .her own need. . .shone out at her from his eyes.

'I love you, Lawrence,' she said slowly and distinctly.

God knew why or how in this short space of time, but it was true. Perhaps it was time she started believing in the miracle of love at first sight. She touched his face.

'And is forever long enough?'

He seemed to stop breathing, as his eyes went on probing hers, but now she had no fear of what he might find.

'Do you love me enough to give up your business?'

he asked thickly. 'Enough to come and live with me here in France. . .in Mill Cottage?'

Kim felt a momentary pang. He was asking her to give up what had once been her entire life. A vision rose, conjured for her cruelly by Pamela, of herself, middle-aged and alone, sitting behind her desk. No Lawrence. . .no love. . .no life.

'I wouldn't have to give it up entirely, would I?' she said tentatively. 'Gordon Brown, my second-in-command, can run it with one hand tied behind his back, as Pam spitefully pointed out to me a lifetime ago. I'm really quite redundant, but there's no reason why I shouldn't keep him on his toes with one or two flying visits occasionally.'

It was hard to let the past go, but Kim had a feeling in her bones that it would get easier.

'No reason I can think of.' Lawrence was smiling, and his eyes gave a warning that his mind was already turning to other, more intriguing thoughts. 'Except that I want a big family, which means you'll be pretty busy most of the time.'

'Oh!' Kim's eyes widened innocently. 'If you want children, then it had better be marriage you're proposing.'

His eyes glittered menacingly. 'What else would I be proposing?'

'I shudder to think.'

He drew her purposefully against him. 'I had it in mind to make you shudder in quite a different kind of way.'

'Stop bragging,' she said, firmly resisting his attempt to kiss her mouth. 'There are a few more words left to say. I haven't heard them yet, and I'm waiting.'

'Come here! I want to devour you,' he growled against her lips.

'Good effort, but not quite.' Kim smiled. It was good, for once, to have the upper hand. It probably wouldn't be a frequent occurrence, so she might as well make the most of it. 'I'll give you a clue. They're short words and there are three of them.'

His eyes narrowed intently on hers. 'I love you, Kimberley Harris,' he said, his voice low and husky. 'Damn you, but I do.'

His lips sought hers again, but with a superhuman effort she resisted.

'That wasn't very romantic,' she complained.

'Then I'll have to practise a little more.'

'Then you'll tell me every day?'

'Probably,' he said, a threatening frown beginning to form between his brows. 'Stop pushing your luck, Kimberley.'

She shook her head. 'Estelle said a Virgo and a Gemini wouldn't make an ideal couple.'

'Estelle doesn't know everything.' He gripped her resolutely. 'And if it's romance you want, how about this for a beginning?'

He kissed her, a slow tantalising kiss, his mouth soft and warm against hers, refusing to be hurried, until she thrust her naked body demandingly against his. His response brought a powerful thrill as he moved to fulfil her.

There was no resisting him now, Kim thought with an intensity of joy, as determinedly he possessed her. Then, there was no room even for thought. On gossamer wings, her heart began to soar.

STARGAZING

YOUR STAR SIGN:
VIRGO (August 24th–September 23rd)

VIRGO is the second of the Earth signs and is ruled by the planet Mercury, which makes you cautious, restrained and practical. You crave order and control in your life and so have a tendency to fuss and criticise, although you find as many faults in yourself as in others. You love children, but you must remember that you can't expect them to be as tidy as you like to be! You are an excellent communicator and have uncanny intuitive powers but your jealousy and possessiveness will often threaten good friendships. Yet you are generous and warm-hearted—despite all the moaning!

Your characteristics in love: Virgoans can seem shy and are often cautious about making the first move in a relationship but, motivated by your desire to love and be loved, you really work hard to keep the magic alive. You expect perfection and tend to nag your partner but you set yourself high standards too and, because you hate deceit in others, you yourself will always be loyal and trustworthy. You believe in the importance of personal privacy and you are happiest if you can keep some degree of space and independence. As a lover, you value touch and togetherness, and sensuality rather than sexuality—but watch out: Virgoan women can suddenly find themselves passionately attracted to the most unlikely men!

Star signs which are compatible with you: You can find harmony with **Taurus**, **Capricorn**, **Cancer** and **Scorpio**—but expect fireworks with **Pisces**, **Sagittarius** and **Gemini**! Partners born under other signs can be compatible, depending on which planets reside in their Houses of Personality and Romance.

What is your star-career? Whatever your chosen career, Virgoans are responsible, efficient, clear-thinking and often workaholics. You enjoy turning chaos into order and so, for an opportunity to display your organising skills and fine discrimination, careers in publishing, administration, education, health, catering, secretarial work or banking should appeal to you.

Your colours and birthstones: Virgoans, with their natural fastidiousness, love the purity of stark white.

One of your birthstones, the dark blue sapphire, is said to act directly on the intellect and is also thought to be subconciously chosen by all those who wish to suppress their emotions, as Virgoans try to do. Another ideal present for a Virgoan woman is sardonyx, from which cameo brooches are made. This stone is said to inspire romance in those who wear it.

VIRGO ASTRO-FACTFILE

Day of the week: Wednesday
Countries: Austria, Norway.
Flowers: Small flowers, hyacinth.
Food: Carrots, celery, apples and raspberries. Virgoans are very health-conscious and prefer to bake, steam or grill rather than fry, and like to use low fat and whole foods in their cooking. But as a treat, you love a fresh cream cake!
Health: As an earth sign you know the importance of exercise and good diet but you can be rather a hypochondriac, so try not to get obsessive about your health!

You share your star sign with these famous names:

Lauren Bacall
Sophia Loren
Twiggy
Shirley Conran
Raquel Welch
Sean Connery
Richard Gere
Roald Dahl
Frederick Forsyth
Michael Jackson